SORROW
SUBLIME

SORROW
SUBLIME

CURTIS L. GRAY

TATE PUBLISHING
AND ENTERPRISES, LLC

Published by Tate Publishing & Enterprises, LLC
127 E. Trade Center Terrace | Mustang, Oklahoma 73064 USA
1.888.361.9473 | www.tatepublishing.com

Tate Publishing is committed to excellence in the publishing industry. The company reflects the philosophy established by the founders, based on Psalm 68:11,
"The Lord gave the word and great was the company of those who published it."

Book design copyright © 2014 by Tate Publishing, LLC. All rights reserved.
Cover design by Rtor Maghuyop
Cover illustration by Jeremy Aaron Moore
Interior design by Joana Quilantang

Published in the United States of America

ISBN: 978-1-63122-555-0
1. Fiction / General
2. Fiction / Fantasy / General
14.03.21

TRUE FRIENDS ARE NEVER STRANGERS

Endowed with the grace of a cat, Moyra Sublime ran along the top of a three-railed fence. The fence was made to keep horses out of the apple orchards it protected. With the little light of early morning, she had to pay more attention to the rails than she normally would. Her comfortable doe-skin shoes were dyed green the same as her threadbare scarf. They allowed her to comfortably adjust her balance without slowing down. The scarf that casually hung over her shoulders wasn't for warmth, but simply to help keep dust out of her face and eyes later in the day. When the highway bustled with wagons, chariots, coaches, carts, and horses, she would always put it to use. Moyra's short red skirt allowed her legs to move freely as she ran. She raveled with joy as she ran over a long narrow rail that bounced and jostled her into giggles. On her way northeast to the city of Brunswick, Moyra often created excitement in little things to pass the time.

The distance of a short bow's range ahead, there were a few wagons on the other side of the road. People were crawling out from under them, where they had slept throughout the night. Others already had a fire going preparing for breakfast. One of the wagons was covered for people to sleep comfortably within. The other wagons were rather large, made to be pulled by six mules each. Most people seemed to still be sleeping. The women in their long dresses and aprons had the look of goodwives. There were many horses beyond the wagons, maybe as many as a hundred. They looked mostly tame but probably unbroken. In between the wagons and horses, there were men taking down tents, rolling them up, and carrying them to the wagons. Few others rode among the horses to keep them from scattering as they grazed.

Missing a step and nearly falling off the fence, Moyra came to a stop, spread her arms, and crouched down low. Then continuing along the fence top at a walk, she was coming to the end of the fence. At which point, she jumped off the corner, landed easily, and turned toward the wagon camp. She had only eaten dried fruit, flat bread, cheese, and tuff jerky the last three days on her way to Brunswick. She was hoping for a hot meal and doubting they would mind feeding one more. She walked up the steep edge of the highway and continued across. Smiling at children as they waved to her, she waved back, coming off the dusty road and into the knee-high grass.

"Good morning," Moyra greeted with a smile to match that of the three women nearest the fire preparing breakfast.

They greeted her warmly by stepping forward to shake hands. The eldest, Mephitis, she named herself, was wearing a bright-green cotton dress down to her ankles and had a wide leather belt that had a silver buckle with flowers carefully etched on it. She had red hair and green eyes like Moyra, though neither where nearly as dark as Moyra's. Mephitis's hair was what Moyra would call strawberry blond and her eyes more a hazel. Moyra had always been told her eyes where a bright emerald green, to which she liked. But she envied Mephitis's darker skin. Even with three days in the bright sunlight, Moyra's skin just burned red but wouldn't tan and would go back to pale milk white in as many days.

The other two wore long dresses of green as well but were faded and less expensive woolen cloth. They were called Bella and Avilla, both young enough to be Mephitis's daughters. Avilla and Bella had the look of sisters, but their dark-brown hair made it less likely they were her daughters. Bella, though younger, was taller and by far the prettier of the two; long full locks of hair hung past her hips and had a seemly wave as though it had recently been in a braid. She kept her dress cleaner and moved with a swift grace that said she was an assertive woman. After introducing each other, Bella's eyes seemed to continue smiling as though she held an amusing secret.

Moyra smiled broadly, feeling she and these women would be fast friends soon for some reason she wasn't sure of. "What is it? Do I still have grass in my hair from just now waking up and I haven't brushed it yet?" Moyra asked, running fingers through her hair and turning to Bella.

All three smiled when Moyra smiled, but when she asked that, Mephitis turned back to the fire and kept working on breakfast still smiling. Bella put on a frown as if her secret had been found out, and Avilla smiled all the wider.

Avilla's hair, shorter than Bella's, only hung halfway down her back; it was much thinner and dull without the gleam of the younger woman's. Even though she was smiling broadly, her eyes didn't smile. Her dress was dirty, and Moyra realized that her hand was at least as callused as her own. Moyra thought she must be a bit of a tomboy and was surprised she wasn't wearing pants instead of a dress.

"No, it isn't that. We were just picking on her about how competitive she is about men she can't even look at another woman without measuring herself against her and trying to find out if men like her better. Her name gives her too big a head if you ask me." Avilla said with a smirk, which earned her a sock on the arm from Bella. The name *Bella* meant "beautiful" and was the name given a queen in an old bard's tale. Bella absently studied her toes in embarrassment, fists still clinched as though she wasn't done pounding her sister yet.

"Very well," Moyra said, smiling again and looking out appraisingly to the men doing different chores as she tapped a finger to her lips. "I am competitive myself, though I can't remember competing in this kind of game before." She swept her eyes mischievously back to Bella, whose eyes were wide in shock. "We will pick out a few men, and whoever they are more smitten with by the time we get to Brunswick wins."

Bella smiled broadly, shaking her head, curling a lock of her hair on two fingers. "You're going to be lots of fun. My sister never even looks at a man who acts interested in me."

Moyra doubted there was a man not interested in Bella; she could have been the muse that inspired men to make all those statues that decorated gardens and bathhouses of the wealthy, which made every woman feel distorted in comparison. Bella finally looked up. With a gleam in her eyes, she said, "Here are the rules: no kissing no telling them what is going on either by word or action. I will pick out two, and you pick out two. When we get to Brunswick, Mephitis and Avilla will judge who they are more 'smitten' with. What do you think? Are you still up to it?" Bella was glowing with the prospect of the idea.

"Oh, I am not shirking out of this. Pick out your two first, then I will pick mine," Moyra said then asked Avilla to bring her a brush, which she happily did. Caught up in the game, she also gathered some small white flowers, which she started putting in Moyra's hair after it was brushed out.

Bella pointed out two young men about four years older than her and Moyra. Moyra locked them into her memory as they put their tent into a nearby wagon. One was tall with messy blond hair; he wore a loose fitting white cotton shirt and was a bit skinny but had an attractive face. The other was short but more attractive to Moyra's eyes, his hair black shorter and in better order, his face just as attractive, if not more stern. He was bare-chested; Moyra guessed he must have slept that way. She let out an exaggerated sigh when he pulled a shirt on, just as loud as need be for it to reach his ears. And she couldn't help but smile with pleasure when he blushed. They were both staring back at her now, speaking quietly to each other. They seemed hesitant to introduce themselves. And she wasn't ready to make it easy on them, so she turned to the fire, knelt, and put some more wood on it, helping prepare breakfast.

Bella let out a small amused laugh when Moyra made the dark-haired one blush. "You're better at this than I expected. It will be a fun challenge." She pointed out some other men now, like a woman picking out race horses she thought likely to win.

Avilla was excited, rubbing her hands together and helpfully telling the little she knew about each new prospect. Moyra thought Avilla saw this as some sort of karma for Bella or maybe revenge for herself. Moyra held no illusions that she was as beautiful as Bella. But she knew full well that her sense of excitement and adventure was a magnetism all its own.

"Have you picked out your two yet?" Bella said as she stirred some diced potatoes. "It's only a short ways to Brunswick I expect we will get there sometime today."

"You're right. We will likely be there a few hours after high sun," Moyra replied, looking to the dawn sun. Without any clouds, it wasn't a very colorful sunrise, so she looked at other men coming in to eat. "What are the names of the two you picked out?" Moyra asked, washing her hands. *Blast it! Look what I got myself into!* Moyra blushed every time another man came into camp. *Come striding into a stranger's camp bold as brass. Now you got flowers on your hair as though you were going courting! Not to mention that's exactly how you're going to act the rest of the day! Fool, silly cabbage-headed fool, you will get no worse than you deserve!* Moyra thought, scolding herself.

"The one in the white shirt is Caleb. The other in the brown linen shirt is Gabriel," Bella replied.

"Those two," Moyra said as she picked up some eggs too help Mephitis add them to the potatoes.

Bella looked from her stirring and cursed when she saw the two young men on horseback talking to Gabriel and Caleb. They looked very much alike, one a little older than the other, but both a year or two younger than Bella. Moyra wondered if Bella was upset because they were younger. The only reason she chose them was they were obviously friends with the other two, and with just one day, she felt she would have to work on them as a group to have a chance of winning. They had the same shade of red hair as Mephitis. Mephitis watched the young men smiling and nodded her approval to Moyra. Moyra decided it was more likely they were Mephitis's sons than Bella and Avilla her daughters. And she had a sinking feeling Mephitis had, in giving her approval, just welcomed her to the family in some small way.

On second glance, Moyra decided she was wrong about their ages. She guessed they must be twins; one was just on a taller horse. That was why she thought he was older than his brother. Both wore green faded short-sleeved woolen shirts, studded leather gauntlets, and black knee-high boots folded down at the tops.

"No, that's not fair! Pick some men our age or older. Did Avilla put you up to those two?" Bella said, gritting her teeth.

"Ah no, she didn't. What do you have against twins?" Moyra asked, passing a plate of food to a smiling gap-toothed man at least fifteen years older than her. She grimaced as he was leaving.

"Nothing, but they are Avilla and my brothers," Bella said in a strained whisper as the four young men came around the fire for breakfast. Moyra noticed the twins had Mephitis's eyes and was glad to see that they stood half a head taller than her, despite being younger. The only thing she could tell apart from them was their weapons. One had a long heavy sword strapped diagonally on his back with a two-handed leather-bound handle over his left shoulder. The other had a dagger on one side of his waist and a sword on the other. Its handle was bound in gray and orange cloth, woven to match that of the dagger.

As everyone picked up a plate of food, Moyra said good morning to each. Caleb and Gabriel warmly welcomed her, but the twins just shyly nodded and took their plates. Then Mephitis gave Moyra a plate for herself, which she took with thanks. Moyra stood and brushed the grass from her sun-burned knees. Again Moyra envied Mephitis's darker complexion. She added the twins to that thought—their tan arms had no sign of sun burn.

"Ah, Moyra, you poor dear, you are burned red as a strawberry," Mephitis said. Noticing her wince as she brushed the grass from her sun burnt knees, she had a pained look in her eyes as she looked Moyra up and down, not unlike that of a mother fussing over a child who hurt herself foolishly. "Bella is your height and build. You can wear one of her dresses. It may be a little loose on the hips…hmm…but you should fill in the rest quite well," she said, taking Moyra by the shoulders and eyeing her as though she were a seamstress planning on making a dress.

Moyra was glad the sun burned her red now, so that the four men, obviously comparing her to Bella, wouldn't see that she was blushing. She twisted out of Mephitis's grasp. "No, thank you. That's okay. Hiding from the sunshine won't do me any good at this point. The damage is all ready done," Moyra said, with a smile of thanks.

"That may be, but you should have worn a longer dress. I know a full-length dress is not as comfortable when you're off adventuring. But with your complexion, you should have at least worn pants," Mephitis said, shaking her head disapprovingly.

Moyra felt a flood of warmth for this motherly woman, who took her in like a stray. She turned to the four men, who were thoughtfully looking from her to Bella then back again. *Blast they are comparing us more openly than Bella ever did*, Moyra thought. *Curse these flowers! They surely think I am here courting now! This short skirt lets them look at my legs all too freely too!* She moved closer to Mephitis, wanting to hide behind her.

"Let's go sit at the back of a wagon to eat. It's getting too warm by the fire," Moyra said, gathering Bella and Avilla as she left the campfire. It was getting rather warm with the sun coming up.

"Now," Bella said, finishing her food and placing the plate with the other two empty ones, "pick two other men. My brothers are not an option." She frowned, crossing her arms below her breasts.

"Ha! You made the rules. If Avilla and your mom say I have to choose again, I will. But otherwise, you're just going to have to be nice to them! And hope they would rather dance with you for the Festival of Seven come nightfall!" Moyra said triumphantly, crossing her own arms below her breasts to show she wouldn't budge on this. Moyra had told them that some friends had written to her, asking her to meet them in Brunswick at an inn called the Dueling Bard on the first day of the Festival of Seven, a celebration of the seven heroes of old of whom bards sung countless songs and told as many unbelievable tales of excitement and intrigue. "I only have one day. This seems a fair handicap. There is no telling how long you have had to win Gabriel and Caleb's affections," Moyra said in even tones.

"Fair is fair, I guess, plus Caleb may start thinking less of me if I start enchanting many men at once," Bella said, and the three young women giggled like little girls.

"Okay, so what are your brother's names?" Moyra asked as she and Avilla walked to the covered wagon and put her pack in the back of it. Bella had left them so she could saddle a horse and ride with the men. Moyra decided to stick with Avilla to learn what she could of them before she started "weaving her enchantment," as Bella called it.

So far Avilla had only talked about Gabriel and Caleb, mostly Gabriel. She seemed to like him better than she knew, "Gabriel this and Gabriel that."

Apparently, they were on the way to Brunswick to sell their horses to be used as the Spearwielder Guard's chariot horses. Gabriel and Caleb had been asked to join the Spearwielder Guard. And they were excited at the prospect of becoming spear-wielding guards of the realm. Moyra could understand that the army pays well, not to mention the promise of adventure and excitement. *I wonder if I could join*, Moyra found herself hoping.

"Their names are Gemini and Echo," Avilla replied. "Gemini wants to become a spear wielder, same as Gabriel and Caleb. But Echo would rather be a mercenary or something like that so he could have more freedom."

Avilla started to tell about her brothers, but Moyra still couldn't tell them apart so she asked, "Wait. Hold on a second. Is there a way you can tell them apart?" Moyra asked. She thought it must be as plain as day to someone who saw them all the time.

"As to that, I can help little, Moyra. Even Mother gets them mixed up most times. And if they don't want you to know, forget it. They may switch weapons or not even wear them." Avilla sounded flustered, muttering something about men and their conniving devices. Much as men do when they find out a woman is up to some mischief.

Moyra laughed; she doubted either one switched anything around; more likely just denied his identity when given a chore that he would rather pass to the other. But Moyra wasn't about to end their fun by suggesting such a thing.

"Well, which one normally wears the broad sword on his back?" she asked instead, adjusting the flowers in her hair.

"That's Gemini. You can't go wrong with him," Avilla said, and it sounded a little bit hopeful. "Besides, I think Echo has his eye on someone else. I am not sure who, but whoever she is, I don't think she encourages him. So she must be older or maybe someone fancy's herself a noble or some such." She was sticking her nose up in the air and looking as though she was looking down on Moyra as she walked. Despite being half a head shorter, they laughed and hugged as they continued to make ready to go.

The wagons started pulling out on to the highway, and the riders had the horse herd moving. Moyra adjusted her scarf so the dust wouldn't get in her face and eyes; it was so thin and threadbare she could still see through it. Avilla seemed to not be bothered by the dust, but Moyra could see that her teeth were already turning brown. They ran to catch up to a wagon and jump on the back. It was too high off the ground for their feet to drag. But as they made their way down the road, they found some sticks to drag behind as they talked.

Later, Moyra found herself riding with Mephitis in the covered wagon because Avilla went rummaging through all the wagons looking for something. And Mephitis wouldn't believe that Moyra wasn't going to start blistering in the sun. But Moyra didn't mind. If her mother hadn't died giving birth to her, she hoped she would have been like this kindly woman. *It may turn out that if I am not careful, I'll end up with Mephitis as my mother in-law*, Moyra thought not unkindly. Mephitis was measuring her for a dress she planned to make for Moyra. She kept telling of her sons virtues, counting them off as she said to stand just so. After Moyra was measured for what she hoped wouldn't be a wedding dress, Avilla came to the wagon waving a large boomerang and asked Moyra to come throw it with her, and Mephitis allowed.

Moyra could remember her father throwing boomerangs quite often recreationally. He said it was for helping him relax and get his mind off work. But she had never seen such a big boomerang as this. The shape looked right to Moyra. Apparently, nobody had gotten it to work yet. And they thought it unlikely that it could turn around by itself and come back.

"I know what it's supposed to do but can't think it really works that well," Avilla said, frowning down at it, then she lobbed it into the air and watched as if she hoped it would start flapping some wings. Moyra laughed and ran to retrieve it; they were well off the highway. The slow-moving wagons had kept going, leaving them behind. But the horse herd was stopped at the Aroostook River not far ahead. There were a few trees on this side of the river but mostly just low rolling hills with grass and prairie dogs. Moyra left her scarf and other things in the wagon because she planned to go swimming. It was getting very hot, so she made her way toward the river as she tried explaining the boomerang to Avilla.

"My father throws boomerangs for fun, but they are lightweight and not much bigger than my hand. It's like watching a slow relaxing juggle. I have never seen one this big—you could probably kill a human with something like this," Moyra said.

Avilla's eyes went wide at that. She had obviously never thought of this toy as a weapon.

"I think the trick is to give it lots of spin, and if you can feel any breeze at all, make sure it is blowing toward your left side. Also, it needs to be upright with only a slight angle. Most beginners try to throw them like a Frisbee, the way you just did. Stand back. This thing may be a bit scary trying to catch if I can get it to come back," Moyra said.

Avilla shook her head doubtfully but moved a few paces back. Moyra spun the boomerang as hard as she could with both hands but otherwise tried to do it just like she had seen her father throw them so many times before. It spun low to the ground at first but gained height and soon started coming back. Moyra was all too aware of the swooping sounds it made, and as it was drawing near, she squawked and found herself running away with Avilla. It hit the ground with a cloud of dust, and they giggled as they gathered it back up again.

They got good enough that they could get it to come back every throw, and Moyra was able to catch it the last time. But she wanted to soak in the cool river before they went the last of the way to the city. Avilla didn't want to go swimming, and apparently nether did Gabriel. He stood well away from the river, skillfully playing a merry tone on a flute. Moyra asked him if he would like to learn to throw the boomerang; he eagerly followed them to the meadow. Moyra decided to only throw it once then leave him alone with Avilla because she was obviously smitten with him, and as an afterthought, she hoped that he would choose Avilla over Bella, which may improve Moyra's chances of winning their game. He stood right at Moyra's side as she threw it. But when it was obvious it was coming back to her, he took Avilla's hand and ran with her to safety. Moyra was laughing so hard she was lucky she was able catch it.

Gabriel had been much closer to her than to Avilla, but Avilla was the only person he was worried about seeing to safety. Thus, Moyra was sure he had some feelings similar to Avilla's for him. With that Moyra, left the pair, Avilla blushed when she realized she would be alone with him. He was quiet and reserved, much the same as Avilla, but he looked stronger than the other three men. Except for being short and not having the gleam in his eye that promised a world of excitement and adventure, he looked very much like someone Moyra hoped to see soon at the Dueling Bard Inn in Brunswick.

The Aroostook River was about as big and wide as a river could be and still be passable by bridge. And yet it still had the fast flow and occasionally white-water rapids of smaller rivers. As for being passable, that was mainly due to the amazing bridge—a testament to hard labor and engineering. To make it, they had built a dam upriver to slow the flow of the river, which caused a village and many farms to be flooded. It also created many lakes, small and large. So that the four pillars could be built, they had sharp points up river to separate the heavy flow of water so that even these massive constructs wouldn't be washed away. The pillars also stood towering over the bridge, holding chains to support the center of each span of bridge on either side. Aroostook was so deep that many seafaring ships could always be seen in the center, away from the edges that periodically had large boulders, which made the river break menacingly in fast-moving rapids.

Moyra walked way down to the river, where Caleb, Gemini, and Echo were taking turns swinging from a tree and dropping in the cool water. The sun was at its highest point, and the heat was sweltering, so Moyra decided to swim in all her clothes so they would keep her cool long after she left the water. She climbed on to a large boulder overhanging the river, ran to the end, and dived in. Oh! It felt good on her sunburns; it felt like two days of burning was instantly taken away.

When her head came up, she was surprised to see how far the river current had taken her downriver. She was surprised to see Mephitis smiling warmly, standing waist deep in the river nearby, with the covered wagon not far off. *I guess just the other wagons continued to Brunswick*, Moyra thought. "Hello, Mephitis, it's good to see you. I thought you went on to Brunswick," she said happily, joining her in slower waters.

"No, I don't have anything to sell in my wagon, and I guessed you and my children would like to have a nice hot lunch. Before continuing on the dusty road, I know my husband expects one," she said, putting her hands on her hips, eyeing Moyra up and down questioningly.

She must be wondering why I swam in my clothes—no, she is wading in her dress. "What is it?" Moyra asked, looking down to see what might be amiss.

"Oh I just noticed your skin is pink now instead of red, like it was this morning. That cold water must be doing you a lot of good," Mephitis replied.

"I envy you. I have never had a tan, but I don't stay red as long as most people, so that's something, I guess." Moyra said, rubbing her hands down her now pink arms and smiling when she looked at her legs. *My skin will be back to snow white by tonight if I stay out of the sun*, she thought happily.

She relaxed with Mephitis only a short time before going to enjoy the swing with the guys. When she got back up where the swing was she found it abandoned. She dropped off the swing a few times but was soon tired from swimming against the current. So she decided to go help make lunch, but when she started that way, she saw Bella.

Bella had her hair in a braid, and she was still dry from head to toe. "Where did every one go" she asked. As she reached out to press an open hand to Moyra's arm, there was a look of wonder on her face at how much the sunburn had gone away.

"I don't know. I was going to help Mephitis make lunch. But I will stay here and swim with you for a bit if you want to drop off the swing a few times," Moyra said companionably.

Bella made a sour face then shook her head. "No, thanks. I was just coming to let everyone know lunch is ready. Here they come. It looks like they figured out the boomerang," Bella said.

Moyra turned around in time to see them scatter as the boomerang started returning all but Echo. He planted his feet then started shifting his weight from one to the other. *He looks like he is ready to run but forcing himself to stay*, Moyra thought. Reaching out both hands, it wacked his left one hard, but he got a grip on it with his right. If he had stepped back, a one-handed grip would have been safe, but he kept his feet planted. The other end of the boomerang came around and cracked his head hard. The sound made Moyra wince with empathy; she turned her head away, knees trembling. When she turned back, she was running to him with Bella at her side. He dropped the boomerang, his knees trembled, and he crumpled to a heap just as they got to him.

She could hear a horse galloping toward them but kept all her attention on Echo. Moyra gently lifted his head and upper back, and then slid her knees under to support him. His hair was wet; she knew it was from the water, not blood, so she had to probe with her fingers to find the cut from the boomerang. *I hope he wasn't trying to show off to me*, she thought bitterly.

The cut was a few inches into the hair line above his left eye, she parted the hair and decided it would need a bandage. As she looked up to ask for a knife to cut the hair by the wound away, she saw that the woman kneeling by her side wasn't anyone from the group but was her dearest friend, Jane Sorrow. *She must have been riding the horse that I heard*, Moyra thought. "Jane, what are you doing here?" Moyra asked wide eyed as Jane

Curtis L. Gray

pulled a dagger and found the place where Moyra was holding Echo's hair away from his now bloody wound.

"I have been riding with them for six days. I told you in my letter that I had been hired as a merchant guard and that I would be in Brunswick by this night and hoped to see you and Cosmos there," Jane said matter-of-factly. She was wearing the long gray-and-orange cloak of her family guild of mercenaries, despite the heat, and soft doeskin clothes with heavy studded leather chaps over her legs, their overlapping plates ending at her knee. Her matching black boots were knee-high, a jerkin of studded leather, to match her gauntlets, which were tucked into her belt. She was well armored for a merchant guard. Her raven-black hair hung just past her elbow, as she finished shaving a small spot in Echo's hair long as a finger.

"Bella, go get a bandage out of the left side of my saddlebag from one of the small side pouches," Jane said, standing and sheathing her dagger.

"Ah...my head," Echo said, trying to raise a dusty hand to his wound, but Jane lightly kicked it away. Moyra held his chin to keep him from getting up then washed his cut with her wet skirt. Then she allowed him to get up so Bella could place the bandage. Gemini made some light banter with Caleb about people knocking themselves out. Everyone laughed, including Echo, who then groaned and put a hand to his head. Bella asked Caleb to help take Echo to the wagon and, as an afterthought, said lunch was ready.

Jane took her horse by the reins. She had the boomerang in her other hand, inspecting it. As she walked to the wagon talking to Moyra, she seemed to like the idea of having a boomerang for a weapon. Jane elbowed Moyra in the side then nodded, pointing with her chin to Avilla walking hand in hand with Gabriel.

I am glad those flowers washed out of my hair into the river, Moyra thought. "Echo sure was determined to catch that boomerang," Moyra said, wondering if he was trying to impress her. *No, he couldn't see me. He was looking up the hill.*

"Aye, if he wasn't trying so hard not to run, he could have taken a few steps back and caught it much more easily," Jane said. Laughing, she gave the boomerang a test swing.

"I didn't know you were watching him. Avilla said he likes an older woman. Your only two years older than me, but that makes four years for Echo. Could you be that older woman?" Moyra said teasingly.

Jane sighed without a hint of blushing, nodding her head. "He would not have tried to catch it if he had not seen me coming this way, I think," Jane said sadly. Taking her reins in hand with the boomerang, Jane lifted Moyra's arm with her other. "It always surprises me how fast you heal. When I saw you yesterday evening, you were red as a beat. When I train with you in hand-to-hand combat, you never bruise. Your red welts and scratches always heal long before mine do too," Jane said with a hint of admiration in both face and voice.

"Why didn't you come and talk to me yesterday if you saw me?" Moyra asked.

"You looked like you were enjoying yourself running along the top of that fence that went around the orchard. Plus it was getting late, and I had some stray horses to bring back. Some peddlers were trying to throw ropes around their necks. I guess we could have ridden double, but I just didn't think of it." Jane gave an apologetic look and hugged Moyra with her free hand. "I am sorry you must have slept poorly out on the grass with that sunburn."

After eating and washing the dishes in the sandbar of the Aroostook River, Moyra asked Mephitis if it would be okay if she slept in the wagon until they got to Brunswick. She replied that Echo was in there because she feared he may have a dizzy spell and fall off his horse. She happily consented. But then as though she had just remembered that Echo already liked Jane, she asked if Moyra would rather have Gemini saddle Echo's horse so she could ride with him.

Is she trying to marry off all her children at once—Bella to Caleb, Avilla to Gabriel, Echo to Jane, and Gemini to me? Moyra let out a long sigh that she tried to disguise as a yawn. With that, Mephitis consented, allowing Moyra some rest.

Moyra crawled into the covered wagon. It was surprisingly roomy. Because the bedding was on top of the other less-used things, Echo was in the back, cutting shavings off a rough piece of wood.

"Hello, Moyra, Bella said you and Jane are good friends. Did Jane say anything about me?" he asked sheepishly. "She has been teaching me how to fight with a sword and dagger like she does." Echo sounded so proud he seemed a few years younger just then, like a student infatuated with his teacher.

Ha! Poor Jane, always too eager to teach. Now she has a teacher's pet, Moyra thought with amusement, guessing he followed Jane around asking questions and looking for her approval in everything he did. "Yes, I have known Jane since she was your age. Did you know she is a twin too?"

Echo's eyes lit up when she told him Jane was a twin like him. He obviously didn't know. Moyra berated herself for telling him that because his look made it feel too much like encouragement. Jane would be mad at Moyra for saying "unnecessary things." Jane said Cosmos would be mad at her for telling Moyra unnecessary things every time Moyra asked about him after only having first met. "They are not identical twins. He is her brother, Cosmos Sorrow. She probably mentioned him."

Echo only nodded, still expecting more.

"Umm…all I can recall she said about you was that you should have taken a few steps back when you caught the boomerang. That way you could have absorbed the impact in your movement, instead of your head," Moyra said, trying to copy Jane's tone when she spoke of him.

He only nodded eagerly too this, as though Jane had shown him how to catch a boomerang.

Moyra shrugged, giving up trying to dissuade him. He was hopelessly smitten with Jane. She lay down. It was still hot in the wagon but not as bad as outside and her wet cloths kept her cool. It was impossible to go to sleep until the wagon got to the highway; the steep hill and grassy plain were just too bumpy. Once on the highway, she nodded off to sleep before the wagon started across the long bridge over Aroostook River. In her dreams, she thought she saw Echo holding a large lump of gold where he had had the block of wood before.

Moyra awoke to the sounds of the city all around. Raising her head, she could see Echo. He had stopped cutting on the piece of wood. It was an unfinished boomerang.

"Hey, Echo, how is your head?" Moyra said, stretching.

"It doesn't hurt as bad as my pride, and I don't get dizzy any more. What do you think of my boomerang? I want to compare it to the other before I finish it, so I get the angles right," Echo said, handing it to Moyra.

"It looks right so far, but why do you need two?" Moyra replied. She started rummaging in her things until she found the comfortable white pleated dress she packed.

"I gave the other to Jane. She was pleased, but I think she thinks of me as a little brother." He looked at Moyra as though he was struggling with himself whether or not to ask her something. "You are obviously not surprised. I know most women want an older, more mature man. You're her best friend. Can you please give me some advice? I will be indebted to you," Echo asked in even tones, but his eyes were pleading.

"Turn your back please. I am going to put this dress on," Moyra said.

He did, but he impatiently drummed his fingers on the boomerang, needing an answer. She hurriedly took her clothes off then started putting on the fresh ones, and then she noticed this wasn't the white dress she thought she packed. It would have to do, but it was much smaller than any other dress or skirt she still owned.

"Normally I would gladly help, but my instincts are the same as Jane's on this. Echo, I'm not trying to be mean. It's just that this feels like infatuation of a student for his teacher, not love." She gave him a hug in apology. He sighed, nodding, but not in agreement, just accepting her reasoning in not helping.

She gathered up her belongings and climbed through the front of the moving wagon to sit at one side of Mephitis. Looking behind the wagon, she was surprised to see they had just entered the city. *I must have woken as soon as we passed the gate*, Moyra thought, surprised she slept so light.

❧

Brunswick was a good-sized city with a wall around it. The city was built against a cliff wall so that they only had to build the city wall on three sides. The cliff was high and stretched miles north and south. People made a few dwellings in the sandstone cliffs but mostly used it to store grain.

"Have we passed any inns on that side of the street yet?" Moyra asked as she looked ahead to see if she could find the next inn. "The Dueling Bard is supposed to be the first on this side, but there are three before it on that side."

"Yes, we passed The Vagrants' Respite Inn, and that next one you're trying to make out should be the Autumn Falls Inn if memory serves." Mephitis said helpfully. "Bella, Gemini, and all the others are still outside of the city. The Spearwielder Guard met us out there. They are taking the horses to their corral. I decided to go ahead and get rooms at the Dueling Bard for my family, just because that's where I was taking you anyway, keeps things simple, unless you object." She raised a questioning eyebrow as they passed a third inn.

"How could I object? All of you have been wonderful. It's been like finding a long-lost family I never knew I had," Moyra said happily, then she hugged Mephitis, her heart rejoicing, tears welling up in her eyes.

Mephitis returned her hug deeply, then patted her on the back and pushed her at arm's length. "True friends are never strangers even when they first meet. Now go inside before you get me crying. Echo will take care of the wagon. I will be right there as soon as I get some fresh clothes," Mephitis said, climbing down after Moyra jumped down to the stone sidewalk to stand in front of the Dueling Bard Inn.

True friends are never strangers, Moyra thought and remembered she predicted much the same thing when she first walked into their camp.

REUNITED SORROWS

The city of Brunswick had a contingent of the Spearwielder Guard at a tower outside the city. The Spearwielder Guard's corral lay bare of horses, as infantry transferred water with buckets from wagon to the short stout barrels. They also placed hay and old carrots that looked like they had spent considerable time in storage along the fence. They hurried about their chores, running to prepare the corral for its new occupants. The dark shapes and growing dust cloud showed that this year's remounts would arrive soon. Finishing up, they drove out of the corral leaving the gates open wide, those on foot climbed over the three railed fence to exit. They were drabbed much like the desert nomads when not in armor. But rather than the cool white clothes that hung loosely to shade and cool the skin beneath, their uniforms were dark blue, almost black, and had a yellow-green emblem of a man with spear and large shield. They carried their shields even less often than they went about in full armor.

There was a light breeze, but it did little to lessen the afternoon heat. The horses coming into the corral were many shades of red and brown. Less than a quarter of them had white ribbons tied on their manes. These, unlike the majority, were not already paid for by the Spearwielder Guard. They where extra brought to sell separately to any one with the coin to pay. These horses were tall, high stepping, and proud as they pranced around, ages ranging from three to seven years old.

Cosmos Sorrow stood at the bottom rail of the three-railed fence. Wearing his guild cloak of gray, with an inside border of orange the outside had orange flames deceptively placed at the bottom. He wore armor of overlapping leather plates studded to hold it firmly together. Many throwing daggers could be seen with expertly woven sheaths in his armor, ready for his grasp, most hung diagonally upside down along his ribs, on leggings, and either arm—all easily accessible. But his main weapons were the double-bladed sword and curved kukris dagger on either hip. He was of average height, dark skinned, raven haired, which is also average, except in the Northern realms, where most everyone seemed to have yellow or white hair.

Watching the riders herd the horses into the corral, he instantly recognized his sister. Jane's long hair as dark as his own hung down to her elbows; she was dressed much the same as he. She even wore the family guild cloak of gray with few orange flames. But her armor didn't cover her as completely, and her tan right arm was bare. She soon noticed him and started around the corral toward him; some of the other riders followed. First, just two women followed; one wore a riding dress split up the center, and the other rode a sidesaddle. When the corral gates closed, three men galloped to join them.

Cosmos waved to his sister, Jane, and laughed when she was the only one of the group not to wave back. She smiled knowingly without looking back to see them waving happily to a stranger. He turned his back to the corral and easily lifted himself to sit on the top rail, with his feet resting on the center rail. As they came closer, he could hear them talking. A man with light-yellow hair grabbed the shoulder of the man nearest him. "Hey, Gabriel, he could be your brother," he said, comparing them.

"Well, I am sure he is not," Jane said, silencing them as they came to a stop in a row in front of Cosmos, who swung his left leg up to the top rail. "This is my twin brother, Cosmos." She climbed down, tied her reins to the fence, then pulled Cosmos's leg off the top rail so she could climb up beside him hip to hip. She put an arm comfortably on his left shoulder, and with the other, she pointed to them one by one. "This one you cannot take your eyes off is Bella," Jane said.

Bella laughed and then blushed crimson when Cosmos smiled and simply continued to stare at her. She was beautiful, long brown hair flowing in waves. He had never seen tan skin that was so smooth. Her smile was contagious, much the same as Moyra's was. He couldn't help but smile when she did. Thinking of Moyra, Cosmos looked around hopefully; Jane had written him saying she would be here soon. They all laughed.

"I am pleased to meet you," Cosmos said, then looking at Jane, he was about to ask after Moyra, but Jane had spoken first.

"Do not worry. Moyra did not see you eyeing another. She is in Brunswick, at the Dueling Bard. You did get us rooms there like I asked, didn't you?" Jane grunted her thanks when he nodded. "This other woman is Avilla, the older of the two sisters. And the one from Salaamed that was staring daggers at you when you were eyeing Bella, he is Caleb." She pointed to the plain woman who had the look of a tomboy, then to the light-yellow haired Northerner, who may have hardened his face some. "This one who could pass for our brother is Gabriel. The last is Gemini. He is a twin like us, but different because they are identical. His brother, Echo, is in town—" Jane smiled teasingly—"with Moyra."

Cosmos decided he wasn't feeling very jealous; he just envied Echo the time he was getting to spend with Moyra. "I brought Moyra's horse, Eclipse. She left him at my place. It is about time I got a horse for myself though, so that is what I am doing down here," Cosmos said, looking over his shoulder to the corralled horses. Moyra had actually given her horse Eclipse to him, but he was sure it meant something in her custom of the people who lived far to the south in the desert. He just didn't know what it was, so as much as he liked the horse, he could not take it.

Gemini was off his horse and walking to the fence when Cosmos looked back to them. He scooped up a bucket on his way. Cosmos jumped down beside him and was surprised the red-headed youth was half a hand taller. He never considered himself tall, but he was sure he was a good four years older than Gemini.

"Cayenne," Gemini said loudly then whistled. A dark red mare came over to him. It had a white ribbon in its mane, marking it as one of the horses not already owned by the guards. "This is Cayenne. I would recommend her to you over all others," he said, proudly feeding the horse a handful of oats he pulled from the bucket.

Cosmos was surprised that the mare came to the call. He had never tried that with Eclipse, but he knew the vivacious steed wasn't that well trained. *Maybe I could give Cayenne to Moyra, and that would make keeping Eclipse okay*, he thought. They haggled on a price for the red mare. Cosmos paid much more then he had planned on. But he didn't expect to get a well-trained horse when he came to the corral. Gemini acted like it was a very cheap price, but Cosmos could tell he was pleased with the deal.

Few other people left the shelter of the cool city to come buy horses. But by the time Cayenne was tied on a lead rope behind Eclipse, the rest of the horses with white ribbons had been sold, most to a horse trainer, so Cosmos guessed that Cayenne's being trained. It was a unique case; some were obviously saddle broke, though not to such an extent. The young white steed was easily excitable. His reins held firm, Eclipse pranced from side to side trying to get a better look at the red mare. Cayenne was content to stay back behind the riderless young Eclipse, flicking her tail in annoyance when the lead rope pulled tight, refusing to indulge to the tugging of the younger horse.

A chariot pulled by four horses came to a stop at a gathering of soldiers not far off. There was a small stone building with a slanted tile roof and a stable in between it and a guard tower. Gabriel and the other two men started that way, talking excitedly of joining the Spearwielder Guard. Cosmos followed the three women. Bella and Avilla seemed quite pleased, saying that Caleb and Gabriel had already been asked to join. Jane sniffed and chuckled too herself, crossing her arms below her breasts as she walked. Cosmos knew she thought little of the guards.

"Abducted!" a spear wielder yelled, stepping off the back of his chariot, shaking in silent rage. He had a short yellow-green braid on his left shoulder, marking him as a captain. Pulling off his helmet and putting it under an arm, it revealed a head of very short black hair. He wore shining half-plate armor, with snug chainmail underneath on his chest and shoulders. Over his armor, he wore a dark blue-violet tabard with yellow-green embroidery of a man holding spear and large shield, the emblem of the Spearwielder Guard.

"Two men seized from the highest camber of the tower!" Pacing back and forth in front of his men, he waved a spear, absentmindedly shaking his head. It was a menacing spear, with an oak shaft as tall as he was a steel point two times as long as an open hand and as wide as a broad sword, armor-rending barbs and, two short points crooked wickedly at either side. It also had a masterfully crafted counterweight on the opposed side of the shaft.

Caleb, Gemini, and Gabriel stopped walking, looking nervously from one another, not wanting to draw attention while it looked like all those soldiers were going to be upbraided.

"Four others killed! Poisoned!" He said *poison* like a curse, spittle flying from his mouth in his rage. He stopped pacing, grounding the butt end of his spear shaft on a beaten grass clump at his feet. "And can you believe what the city council said when I told them this? Rather than send word to the capital asking for reinforcements to be sent and placed under my command, they asked me to resign, threatened to discharge me."

Jane walked past Gabriel and the other two men, continuing straight toward the irate captain. Cosmos stepped closer to her protectively walking by her side, Bella and her sister waited with the others.

"It is good to see you again, Cosmos. I fear Moyra plans on asking you to go home to the desert with her when she leaves. If you go south with her, it may be years before I see you again." Cosmos had been planning on going south just before Jane had asked him to meet her here in Brunswick. She said Moyra was coming to Brunswick also, or he would have headed south regardless.

"I think I would like to see her home but, I am not in a hurry to go" said Cosmos.

Jane laughed at him; she knew him better than that. He couldn't pull the wool over her eyes so easily. She obviously knew he was anxious to see the lands that the enigma called Moyra Sublime came from.

"Besides, you said you liked it there. What is keeping you from going back?" Cosmos asked.

Jane had spent three years in the desert with Moyra as her bodyguard. Her father, a feudal lord, had been in a civil war over who would control the Sands Holding salt mines. Cosmos was sure he would miss her if he was gone nearly that long. But he had hoped she might be willing to go south too, even if only for a short time, to show him around a little.

Jane smiled a toothy grin as they neared the captain. She probably thought she was reassuring Cosmos. He grimaced and put a hand on either weapon at each side of his waist. She was the guild of mercenaries champion and always seemed to find reasons to duel. She wasn't likely to do anything too rash, but he knew she was impetuous like him, always acting on the spur of the moment, though he considered her more likely to do something reckless than he was.

"They asked, 'how can the good citizens of Brunswick expect us to protect them?'" Captain Sanders asked, spreading his arms wide. "When spear wielders are being abducted from our guard tower, carried away in the night to who knows where like mice in an owl's talons, they think doubling our numbers will be too costly and posting archers on every roof top ineffective."

Cosmos thought he knew what this man was talking about. In the two days he had spent in Brunswick waiting for Jane and Moyra, he heard rumors of demons or giant bats flying to the highest buildings and taking people from the top floors. Anyone who tried to stop them were cursed or poisoned. They died before morning of their inflictions, but very few were killed because whenever somebody was taken away, it was usually in stealth. One man said when he was coming home from a tavern, he looked up from the street and saw giant bats landing on his balcony. By the time he got some guards to come search, his servants were missing and there were hardly any signs of a struggle. Two streets over people heard a scream as they looked up. One of the monsters dropped his servant she fell and broke her neck.

"Captain Sanders," Jane said, stopping beside him. Cosmos looked askance to Jane, but she kept her attention on the spear wielder. He was in his late thirties, no taller than Cosmos, but more conspicuous in his padding and shiny armor. His big nose and high cheeks were sunburned, but he had white lines around his eyes from always squinting when the sun was on his face.

"What is it you want?" he asked. He didn't sound angry anymore, but impatience was clear on his face.

"I have been hired to help Brunswick during the crisis of these abductions." She handed him a small dark-blue scroll with yellow-green ends.

"And what help might you provide? I recognize those mercenary guild cloaks. Bah! That guild is nothing but a den of assassins." He took the scroll and pushed one end in a belt pouch without reading it.

"That depends on how much you already know of these abductors and what you're doing about them. A group I was with got attacked by some of them a few weeks ago. When we were camping, they glided down from a high cleft in the eastern walls of the cliffs," Jane explained

Cosmos watched the captain's face go from wonder to shock then back to wonder as he listened. He fingered the scroll that stuck half out of his pouch as she spoke. Then when she said they came from the eastern cliffs, he looked that way, as if he half-expected to see something gliding toward them on wings of shadow.

"Hello, I am Gabriel, and this is Caleb. We have been asked to join the Spearwielder Guard."

Captain Sanders looked at the group who just joined Jane and Cosmos, then to Jane in askance. When she said nothing, he fingered the scroll as though he was itching to read it. He was probably wondering if this was the group that was attacked, thinking how he can gain an advantage without giving one to Jane.

Gabriel continued. "These two, Gemini and Avilla, would also like to join. Though neither has been formally asked to join, they hope to become spear wielders."

Jane frowned, shaking her head and looking down in disappointment. Cosmos knew she couldn't see why anyone would give up their freedom to join an army.

"Well, I'm pleased to accept you four into the Spearwielder Guard. I am Capt. Jerald Sanders," he said with a smirk, probably thinking he had gained something from Jane she wasn't willing to part with and was possibly correct.

"Thank you very much. We will be in your care," all four said in unison and then bowed deeply.

Jerald motioned someone over and had them escorted to the guard tower so they could sign up as new recruits, adding that they would have to get and pay for their own rooms in Brunswick until after the Festival of Seven, after which, they could stay in the city barracks with the other soldiers. The reason for this was Salaamed, their sister realm, had a navy ship anchored in the river. After four months at sea, rather than sail all the way around the continent, they were returning home by way of the Aroostook River and stopped for a much-needed rest. But because of the festival, the Brunswick city council had them share the city barracks, fearing rough and rowdy seamen would disturb the festivities, plus they wanted the inns open for citizens coming for the Festival of Seven.

"It's the poison they use that puts my hackles up. No man should have to die like that," Jerald said then shivered and worked his mouth as though just thinking about it had made him dry mouthed.

"They use two types of poison as far as we know, sleeping poison for their captives and powerful, cruel killing poison of anguish," Jane said with tears in her eyes, making them glassy. She hugged herself. Bella came between her and Cosmos, putting an arm around Jane and rubbing the shivers out of her.

Cosmos and Jane had seen people tortured, but she always took it well. He wondered how the memory of something could affect her worse than that had. This must be a very nasty poison; the malice that someone would have to have for them to use it would be repugnant. He guessed that she could have been good friends with the group that was attacked. Watching friends die or convulse in a poisoned fever would be no easier than sitting at the sick bed of a loved one while they died.

"People that got the pain poison had fevers like most minor poisons. But the worst of it was excruciating beyond relief, bone-breaking muscle spasms," Jane continued more calmly but with a far-off look in her eyes. "They couldn't even talk. Jason clinched his teeth so tight they chipped and broke. Terry started off crouched in a ball, rocking on his heels and hugging himself. Once the spasms started, he crushed the ribs in his chest, muscles squeezing harder than your body is normally able too."

Bella gasped, and suddenly Jane was the one comforting her. "And these monsters are here attacking the city regularly?" Bella asked, glad for the solace Jane was providing.

"They are not demons or giant monstrous bats like the rumors say—" Jane tried to explain, but Jerald interrupted.

"How many of your group did they take? How did you escape?" Jerald asked, eager for the rest of the story. He stepped in front of Jane to bar her way as though he thought she would hurry Bella away, take her to her parents, and assure everyone that the city was safe, telling them that they must be different monsters, that they were only rumors, not real danger. More than that, he was afraid she would leave without giving him all the information she had on the abductors. He was the type who would squeeze everything out of an informant and give nothing in return.

"Bella, go to the city. I am sure your mother has acquired rooms by this time. Try looking at the Dueling Bard. That's where Moyra, Cosmos, and I are staying. She will likely try to put the rest of you under the same roof as us," Jane said, urging Bella back toward the horses. She left after making Jane promise to tell her the whole story later.

"Now tell me the whole story. How did you survive? Did you play dead and just let them leave with your friends?" Jerald said scornfully.

"I don't like your tone. You may be a captain, but you have no command over her! And you show great disrespect to her and those who asked her to come help this city in its time of need," Cosmos said, stepping in between Jane and Jerald. Jerald seemed more and more the pompous fool; Cosmos and Jane felt spear wielders in general were all too pretentious. Hundreds of years ago, when the Spearwielder Guard was just a young new army, it might have had strived to be the "example of excellence." But now its bulging numbers were the only thing raising it above other kingdom's armies. The army was a reflection of the realm—spoiled and wealthy. Other realms overindulged them because Lorneoin made them wealthy as well. Lorneoin was an overripe fruit spoiling those touching it—one bad apple spoils the barrel.

"Cosmos," Jane interrupted, putting a hand on his shoulder. "I had no intention of telling him anymore until I have some idea what they know."

Jerald stuck his nose in the air and crossed his arms like a child who had just been snubbed. Cosmos and Jane looked at each other and laughed at the silly stance. It was a comical stance for him to take and seemed ridiculous, even juvenile. Jerald looked down, abashed at their amusement. Cosmos knew he himself would be mortified if he had ever acted that way, unless he had done it just to make people laugh. Jerald, a good fifteen years older than them, looked genuinely ashamed.

Cosmos thought he must have been raised with a lot of sisters or maybe as a lord. Some people walk around with their nose in the air all their life if they have lived a sheltered life. One of Cosmos's friends, Terry, had six older sisters, and they all treated him like a little prince. Protected from the unpleasant, upsetting, and testing experiences of life, he often took that very stance.

"How 'bout that? He could have been the very image of Terry when something did not go like he thought it should," Cosmos said then wished he hadn't when he saw Jane look so defeated. She had just said Terry died, crushed his ribs in on himself during a violent attack of muscle spasms. "I am sorry, Jane, I did not know that it was the same Terry you just told us had been poisoned." Terry was snobby and patronizing; Jane got along much better with him than Cosmos did. That may have been because she acted a little lofty herself. But Cosmos suspected his twin sister, Jane, of having deeper feelings for Terry.

"It is okay, Cosmos," she said then turned to Jerald. "Captain Sanders, have you and your men killed or captured any of these abductors?" Jane gave him a steady look that said she expected a forthcoming answer.

"They kill anyone who sees them up close. Up until last night, I don't think any have been killed. I think my men may have killed four, judging by the amount of blood in the tower. But they carried away their dead and injured, if that is the case," Jerald replied, then shook his head as though thinking of something that didn't make sense to him. "But this isn't like them. The historical scrolls say they abducted beggars and homeless from the streets years ago. But now they don't touch the ground there, just taking people from the highest buildings and only from the top of them, coming and going fast, avoiding confrontation. A lot of people have seen them from the ground, myself included. They are large bats as big as a human. Their wings span twice that. Their heads look like that of a fox, instead of the big flat pig nose of a bat."

"No. That description is accurate—but at the same time all wrong. You are only seeing what they want you to see. I wanted to hear that you had captured one. The one we captured didn't live until morning."

"What? You're going to tell me you didn't just survive but your group managed to capture one of those monsters?" He was shaking his head incredulously.

"You are a real laugh." Cosmos chuckled. "You just now said that you think four were killed last night. Now you act like no one else could have had that much or more success. Why don't you listen for a minute and maybe you will learn something? It is not like a bigger, better-trained group could not overwhelm a group of them." Cosmos smiled at him as he pointed at the guard tower but didn't give him a chance to interrupt. "Yes, I know you said they attacked the tower. But I will eat my boots if it was not a short skirmish that did not end before help could arrive."

Cosmos watched Jerald and wondered if he would just get mad or if he would think back on the attack and come to a reasonable conclusion. At first he was red faced, far more than the sunburn justified, then it was as if wheels were turning in his head. Cosmos knew he was ready to divulge more of what happened in the guard tower last night.

Whenever Jane brought him into conversations like this, he knew his role. He was supposed to gather information by being the astute observer. Some people talk freely; in those cases, he would just remain silent and listen to everything. Other people gave more away by their facial expressions than anything they would openly divulge. Then there were those who expected you to be like an open book, treating you as though you were being interrogated, poking and prodding, probing without sharing what they knew. Cosmos saw a gleam in Jane's eyes and realized she liked him being condescending to the captain. But he felt regret for his haughty actions. He decided that was one reason why she had liked Terry so much more than he did. That arrogant behavior—or confidence, whatever she would call—it must be appealing on some level to her.

"You're right. The men in that room up there were asleep, and many didn't wake up until morning. They used the sleeping poison on them but left all but two because they wouldn't take them over their own dead and injured," Jerald said, scratching his chin thoughtfully, like he was just now putting it together. "They used killing poison on the four men who tried to stop them, including my best man." He was very tensed, and his eyes had a glassy glaze, much the same as Jane had been when she spoke of the pain poison.

"He was screaming in pain when I came in a piercing cry. He had already broken a leg by thrashing against the wall and pulled an arm out of socket. He arched his back so fast and hard he knocked me off my feet as I tried to help him. When I stood up, all was quieted," Jerald said. He was shivering, but sweat was coming down his face in the afternoon heat. "When I stood up, I saw that he crushed his head against the stone wall, mercifully putting an end to those agonized, unbearable, tortured screams. Finally, he just lay there, bones penetrating flesh and blood bleeding out onto the floor."

Cosmos could understand that Jerald's morale had gone low by the way his men died. Many solders could fight knowing they would die on someone's blade, but poison would be like a phobia to them. They couldn't fight back against it any more than they could with sickness. Even if you had an antitoxin, you'd be fighting time more than anything else. It's disheartening to all those nearby, and that could be the very reason the guard tower was attacked. Demoralizing the defenders makes for a weaker opponent; surely, two abductions weren't worth four deaths of their own.

"When they attacked us, I think they were overconfident from their great success against the city or maybe desperate, but I do not know why, unless they feared we might find a weakness and exploit it," Jane said.

"Overconfident maybe, but I don't think so, unless they are much slower flying away from the ground," Jerald said thoughtfully.

"They do not fly." Jane laughed. Cosmos thought she must find it very funny that her one encounter taught more than an entire city learned from months of abductions. "They glide something like a leaf falling from a tree, which is why they only take people from the highest buildings. If they land too low, they would have no chance of getting over the city wall," Jane explained.

"That can't be! Because years ago, they took people, but they were taking them from the ground the streets. Much fewer were seen, but everything I have read describes them the same in appearance. There were some sketches, drawings of them—bat head, ears, and eyes, long snout like a fox, and a red furry mane sort of a cowl, kind of like a lion's mane, but much smaller and red, sometimes black or brown. They were human sized, but from what I could find, nobody saw them fly like we all have now." Jerald now sounded exasperated, as though he had been repeating himself. Maybe he had told people what he knew of them many times today.

"I read some of those scrolls back at the guild when we were trying to find out who attacked us. When they were taking people from the ground all those years ago, the wall around Brunswick had not yet been complete. They are humans dressed like bats," Jane said. Jerald looked like he would argue, but Jane waved down his protests before he could get a word in. "Trust me, Captain, we pulled bat-head helmets off the six men that attacked our group. So I know they are not bats, and I know they cannot fly. Their wings are just a large frame with hinges and strong black silk on it that folds up when they pull their arms down. I brought helmets and winged gliders. They are in a wagon in Brunswick right now."

"So did you kill them all or capture some of them?" Jerald asked.

But Jane pointedly ignored the question, crossing her arms under her breasts. "I think it is time you read that scroll. When I was hired, I wrote a letter to the Obsidian Throne in the capital city of Gara, asking permission to challenge for the Spear of Command. That scroll is the reply from the monarch of Lorneoin, King Sebastian Otogha," Jane said.

Cosmos could feel himself go still in shock of hearing that Jane intended to make a challenge for the spear of command. Jerald stumbled a few feet back; his astonishment was like a kick in the teeth. Challenging for the spear used to be common place among the Spearwielder Guard as a way to keep their skills sharp. An officer could lose command in part just by losing a duel. To take full command, you would have to prove your skill in many tests of tactics, guile, and astuteness. But Cosmos had never heard of a mercenary challenging for command.

The Spearwielder Guard had always been the ideal, perfect army of Lorneoin, and their numbers were so high they didn't need mercenaries. Just about the only use for mercenaries in Lorneoin would be as merchant guards. But they'd find jobs few and far between because the Spearwielder Guard guards for merchants as often as not. Mercenary numbers would dwindle, except in times of war. But the family guild stayed afloat by taking bounties for bands of bandits that would cross borders between realms and guarding merchants who did the same. The Spearwielder Guard and other armies seldom crossed realm borders.

SPEAR OF COMMAND

"So you wish to duel me for partial command, is that it?" Jerald asked, outraged, as he unrolled the small dark-blue scroll Jane had given him.

"Yes. The Brunswick City Council hired me and asked that I send a letter to the capital city of Gara asking for permission to challenge for the Spear of Command," Jane said calmly, like dueling for dominance was an everyday accordance that everyone should adhere too.

"Ha! Ha! This says that if I don't believe you to be my equal, I can have you fight my second before I have too accept your challenge!" Jerald said triumphantly.

"That is acceptable, but it also allows me a second. Cosmos, are you willing to duel his second to prove my effectiveness?" Jane asked.

"Umm…sure, Jane, but he said his best man died last night defending the guard tower," Cosmos replied looking down to the west as the sunset was coloring the horizon. Dusk was always his favorite time of day. He preferred sunset to sunrise because it looked more awash in vibrant reds and oranges. Some people say dawn is just as nice, but he didn't think sunrise was as full of liveliness or energy. Cosmos liked dueling all right, but it was more Jane's thing. Given the choice, he would just as soon go hunting or any sport rather than dueling.

"My second could defeat four men at once. If you do that and convince me Jane is better than you, then I must accept her challenge, but I think you are the better fighter. Few women place much importance in fighting skill." Jerald said incredulously as he apprised the two of them.

"I assure you my sister sees combat as a prime importance, effectiveness, or prominence. Furthermore, she wins four out of five duels against me," Cosmos said, still looking west as the sunset made colors reds, blues, and purples dance across the Aroostook River.

Jane smiled. "I would say nine out of ten duels, but it does not matter. Just pick the four you will send against him. I want to get this over with before dark."

Cosmos nodded his head, silently agreeing with her about her winning nine out of ten duels against him. It wasn't that she was that much better than him. It's just that he couldn't make himself fight his sister as hard as he would some other foe or antagonist. If anyone asked, he knew she would concede, if reluctantly, that he had a better defense than her. He could keep her from get-

Curtis L. Gray

ting a good hit in indefinitely as long as he didn't lose patience and make a careless attack.

"It will take some time for them too put on their armor. You are both armored, and that is just as well. We will not be using wooden practice weapons for a formal challenge, though it would be folly for you to kill any of my men," Jerald said as he turned and pointed out four men seemingly at random. But Cosmos knew he was picking men he considered good fighters; otherwise, he would have chosen the few men already in armor. Jerald jogged to the guard tower with the four men he asked to go put on their armor, obviously giving them last-minute combat tips.

"Be careful. I fear they will have no reservations about killing you or me," Jane said as she took off her cloak and motioned for Cosmos to do the same. "They may try and wound you badly, but if you are obviously winning, I do not think they intend on killing you, except under the circumstances that you allow it to look like an accident or that you are so obviously over-whelmed that not killing a would-be usurper would be insulting." She took his cloak from him and placed a boomerang she pulled off her back in between his cloak and hers. Cosmos didn't like being called a usurper; he was gaining nothing from the fight to come. Jane was the only one who would have any say in how the Spearwielder Guard came against these agents of dark-ness, or "abductors," as they were coming to be called.

"Wow, that is a big boomerang. Is it lethal against a person?" Cosmos asked. He had never seen her carry one before. Smaller boomerangs were commonplace.

People use them to kill small rodents, rats, squirrels or marmot, and often carrion-eating birds that make mischief of themselves by spreading garbage and trash before it gets burned or buried.

"I believe it could be an effective weapon. Gemini's twin brother, Echo, knocked himself out with it, even after he had it in hand. So surely, it would do even better if it hit someone before coming back."

"They are coming back now. Are you sure you don't want to fight all five of them?" Cosmos said, jokingly. "I think the four of them will likely fight better than Captain Sanders."

"I think so too, but I would wear myself out fighting them while trying not to kill them at the same time. You have always been better at staying your blades, though I doubt you have fought more than one spear wielder at once," Jane replied evenly.

She was right. Back home at the guild, the weapon masters intrigued themselves by pitting Cosmos against several foes at once. But he couldn't remember going against several people using spears. It was normally against all swords but sometimes mixed weapons.

"Just keep the distance between you and them closed. Spears are next to useless in close corridors," Jane reminded him.

"Yes, but we are outdoors, unless they are stupid they will stay away from each other so they can guard each other. I will be easy meat if they know how to work together," Cosmos said, wishing they could duel indoors.

"They are preparing an encirclement. It is large, favoring their spears' reach. If their teamwork is good, just fight with your back at the border, then they cannot surround you." Jane pointed to an area where guards were gathering.

"Are you ready, boy?" Captain Sanders asked in a mocking tone.

"I suppose," Cosmos said.

Walking to the center of a large circle the soldiers had cleared and outlined by a thick red-and-white rope that lay on the ground in a perfect circle. He knew he had to cut down their numbers fast before they had time to coordinate a good attack plan. He also knew from his vast experience of group fighting that he had to take out the weakest links first. His teachers had always told him that he was good at measuring up his opponents and that he must trust himself and go with his instincts.

"The rules are as follows," an unarmed solder spoke loudly. "An opponent must drop his or her weapons if blood is drawn in a critical place—head, neck, or chest, if the attack could have hit the heart. Anyone who attacks someone after they willingly drop their weapon is subject to judgment. If anyone is killed, it will count as lack of control against the attacker, thus failing and losing. Only the most controlled and disciplined fighter deserves to count their self a worthy adversary in this contest for the Spear of Command." He continued on about not crossing the border and the honorable history of dueling for the Spear of Command.

As he finished, four armed and armored men brazenly entered the circle. Two were tall, one was of average height, and one was short. They were armored in half-plate armor like the captain, and they all wore helmets. Of the taller two, Cosmos marked the weakest link. The guard stumbled over the large red-and-white perimeter rope while adjusting his shield. He was a head taller than Cosmos but thinner; he probably was not any heavier despite his height. He also had long fine golden hair coming out of his helm, hanging past his shoulders. Cosmos marked the shortest one as the next weakest link because he dragged his spear along the ground like a child with a half-forgotten toy. He obviously didn't take this seriously even if he was very skilled. Underestimating an unknown foe was a weakness Cosmos intended to exploit. It was harder to guess the skill of the last two. The tall one was far stronger and intimidating; the other was older, likely experienced; Cosmos wasn't ready to presume too much. They both moved with a menacing grace.

Suddenly Cosmos had a dagger in each hand, throwing them at each of the two combatants he had not yet placed in the proverbial chain. The older one slapped away the dagger that was aimed at him. The other simply watched the dagger aimed at him and didn't flinch as it bounced inoffensively off his breast plate. He still could not place an order in the chain as to which of them was the weaker link. They were all just out of slashing range with their spears now. Cosmos remembered what Jane said. "If you are so obviously overwhelmed, not killing a usurper would be insulting." He decided to try and use that against them to get them to attack rashly.

He mentally prepared himself for combat, like the weapon masters had instructed him so many times at

Curtis L. Gray

the guild. He let all his emotions drift away distant and unobtrusive to the edge of his consciousness. At the same time, he embraced his senses, hearing their breathing and his own, feeling his heartbeat throughout his body, seeing each of their individual movements, smelling a slight hint of fear on the tall, skinny one. One of the weapon masters describe this as dropping a second skin, removing a metaphysical container, or astral projecting your awareness to encompass a wider area. It was like a rush of adrenalin telling you that you could do anything. In that moment, the euphoria that he felt was beyond ecstasy; he knew he would chase the feeling of jubilation, seek it wherever it could be found for no other reason than the pure exhilaration of it. *This must be why Jane is so addicted to combat*, he thought not for the first time.

Cosmos shook a little, imitating fear. He took a purposely clumsy step backward, making it look like he twisted his ankle. He fell, pulling sword and dagger at the same time. His blades were tarnished and water-stained gray cold steel, not polished and made to shine like silver as so many blades are. Three of them rushed at him, stabbing spear points at him. He was sure all three were going for the kill.

He quickly lifted himself up and forward over three spears that were now stabbed into the ground where he had been. He brought his sword to the throat of the youngest of them to his right, drawing a small line of blood; at the same time, he stabbed his dagger under the left arm of the tall, skinny one. The dagger hit the chainmail at the seam, but he forced it in and stopped it before it could find his heart. He then jumped back as the fourth man thrust his spear at Cosmos's heart. At the same time, the older man thrust his fist out, opening his palm. A yellow cloud formed where his head had been. The cloud spread fast and hung in the air. Cosmos knew it was some kind of blinding powder and was glad it missed his eyes.

The tall man with long thin golden hair dropped his spear. Placing his right hand to the bloody place under his shield arm, eyes bulging with shock, he dropped to his knees. As he stared in amazement at his blood-soaked fingers, some of the blinding powder got in his eyes. He raised a shaky left hand to them, bumping himself in the head with his shield.

The short young man looked down at him then put a hand to his own neck as though he hadn't known he was bleeding too. The other tall man who had broad shoulders grabbed his spear from him before he could drop it.

The assembly of soldiers roared. Some had laughed at his feint when he fell down. But they kept their silence now, as Cosmos was in the critical-defenses stance. He deftly blocked every attack of the older man. He dexterously circled him, trying to get the other man to move in beside him, but he wisely stayed a spear's length away so that he could properly guard him if Cosmos got too close. Cosmos noted that Gabriel, Caleb, Gemini, and Avilla were crowded around Jane, looking over her shoulders or scrunched up against her to make room for all the new people coming to watch.

"Fall back and guard me. I will take him!" the taller man said in frustration of not being able to circle as fast as need be to attack Cosmos at the same time as the other man.

Cosmos rushed at him as he backed away, trying to get a critical hit in and not wanting him to have a chance to rest while Cosmos was forced to fight the other man. The tall man didn't give him the chance, throwing the spear he took from the short guy, effectively stopping Cosmos.

This man's long spear point was on a flexible shaft unlike the others that were all rigid on hard wood shafts. As it quickly arched through the air stretching for Cosmos throat, he had to nimbly roll to his right. He was now certain this man was the best spear wielder of the four, so he entered the aggressive-refrain stance. Cosmos now embraced his celestial sphere, his incorporeal being, the astral projection of his ethereal self. He could feel his skin go cold and his palms sweat, his breathing steadied. Dodging the spear became easier, but he never moved more than he had too to avoid it. The tall man's eyes grew wide as he backed away from Cosmos's blades coming at him in a flurry. He would block the dagger only to have to jump back from a sword trust at his throat. The flood of motion overwhelmed him, even when the other man thrust his spear at Cosmos. It was to no avail. He simply deflected it toward his opponent or was no longer there. Aggressive refrain was a taxing stance if you stayed in it too long, requiring too much strength and precision.

Cosmos battered his adversary mercilessly, putting dent after dent in his rival's breastplate and shield. The tall man adjusted his spear to wield it like a quarterstaff and dropped his shield. He went into the whirling-defense stance, rotating and effectively blocking all attacks against him, sometimes knocking Cosmos off balance. He bashed him in the ribs with the end of his spear shaft then the knee. Cosmos blocked few more than half the attacks but made sure to keep the spear tips from hitting him. The spinning of his opponent was disorienting while astral projecting; the arcane aura around Cosmos shimmered and started to fade.

Cosmos entered rain on sand, a stance that looked like aggressive refrain to the untrained eye. But the attacks were more random; they aimed for arms and legs more often and were less forceful. He made the older man his target now that the tall man wielded his spear like a quarterstaff. He would have to fight dangerously close to his ally if they intended to collaborate with their efforts.

The older man was still winded, but he came at Cosmos in abandon, gaining a second wind. Cosmos danced back from an impaling charge, allowing the two of them to join up, then he darted forward. He rolled on his left shoulder ducking under the spear. As he came to a crouching position, he stabbed the left leg three times fast with his dagger but only got one hit in the right leg with his sword. The attacks barely drew blood through his chainmail, but they would slow him down.

The second spear came for his face, but he rolled back to his back, then swiped it out of the way with his sword. He arched his back, bringing his legs over his head and snapping them back, throwing himself to his feet, then he swung his sword at the tall man's face

Curtis L. Gray

forcing him to jump back. Cosmos also jumped back, engaging combat against the older man. He thrust his dagger at his heart under the left arm, but it must have been expected because his elbow came down hard, knocking the thrust away. Then bringing the shaft of the spear strait at his face, Cosmos leaned as far to his right as he could, following through with a one-handed cartwheel on his sword hand. He hovered for a second with his legs straight up then. Gracefully coming to his feet Cosmos smiled—it was a move marked by poise. Jane would be proud.

Someone clapped excitedly as though the combatants were performers. Another gasped. Cosmos looked around and found it was Avilla. He blushed, feeling egotistical or narcissistic.

"Come get some!" Cosmos taunted, dragging his dagger down his sword blade, then doing the same with his sword down his dagger making scraping metal sounds.

"I'll hit you like a landslide!" the tall man yelled then charged, swinging the spear over his head a few times, then bringing it down to point at Cosmos heart as he boldly, carelessly charged.

Cosmos could feel his blood heating, his metaphysical awareness tipping to one side. He knew he would have to be careful. The arcane aura or insubstantial ethereal presence must be balanced, or you could go into a raging frenzy. The idea is to distance yourself from emotions, not forget them; by forgetting them, you bring yourself closer to opposed emotions you're less aware of. Rage's opposite is fear. So Cosmos stretched his incorporeal consciousness toward fear to make a balance, like extending your arms would help keep your balance while standing on top of a tall, narrow pole.

Cosmos took two running steps toward the other man's charge and leaped into the air. The spear came up to meet him, but the toe of his left foot pressed down on it as he passed over, kicking his right foot forward just in time to meet the charge, knocking the wind out of him. But the heavier man kept his momentum, sweeping the feet out from under Cosmos. He spilled forward, crashing to the ground head over heels. The older man was suddenly there, spear swiping down. Cosmos got his sword up to block, but after his tumble, his grip wasn't sure yet. The attack deflected wide but carried the sword with it, knocking it out of Cosmos's hand.

Cosmos rolled forward from his sitting position and stood, turning to face his foes back. As he stood, he wrapped his right hand around the older man's chest, pulling him hard against his chest. With his left hand, he drew a small line of blood at the neck with his dagger and told him to drop his spear. After that, Cosmos started toward his lost sword but had to draw a second dagger to fend off a barrage of relentless attacks from the tall man. The menacing onslaught was very fast and hard hitting, so much so that he had to pull a third dagger and hold them backhanded. Because one of them had been knocked out of his hand already, his hand stung from the vibrations, like hitting an anvil with a heavy hammer without gloves on. He decided this must be a spear wielder's version of aggressive refrain. The best defense against it was whirling defense.

Unfortunately, it was just as disorienting for him to fight while maintaining his astral projection, and for some reason, it was especially hard to balance his aura today. Not simply because he was a better fighter and did not fear his opponent, but more like his opponents rage was infectious. So Cosmos kept his stance rain on sand, trying to score minor hits, because he didn't think he could keep astral projecting in a more defensive stance.

Cosmos ducked under a heavy swing then used the momentum to twist along the shaft of the spear to get close so he could use the daggers for more than just defense. His left-hand dagger hit hard against his opponent's helm, but not drawing any blood wouldn't end this contest. The hit should have dazed the tall man, but his eyes only showed rage. As he finished the spin, his right-hand dagger angled a little lower to cut along the neck. But his big, tall angry opponent hit Cosmos in the face. It looked like he was going to punch him, but suddenly his fist was open. As Cosmos stumbled backward, he realized the palm that slammed him in the face was full of the yellow blinding powder. He stumbled backward, waving his daggers as fast as he could in front of him.

Suddenly Cosmos felt fear wash over him. It was thick and cold; his astral being was choking on fear. These people were trying to kill him—now that he was blind, the last one of them would surly succeed. He let fear go, but now that he was afraid—truly had something to be frightened of—it wouldn't leave him. With rage and fear pulling on him equally, the metaphysical balance steadied. His astral projection poured energy into him. Immersed in the ice-cool energy of fear and the steaming hot energy of rage, he entered a defensive stance.

He could hear people cheer and others groan in disappointment. The crowd knew it was over; a blind man didn't have a chance of winning. His eyes burned in pain from the blinding powder. Salty tears poured in abundance as he futilely tried to clear his sight, hastily blinking his eyes.

Amazingly, Cosmos blocked attack after attack as he danced backward. Without astral projection, it would be impossible; miraculously, he could feel the spear every time it invaded his space. It was a distant thought until invading the area of his near aura, and then he could feel it cutting toward him. He relied deeply on his hearing to every step, breath, and especially the swoosh of the spear. As he nimbly danced away, he would frequently throw a dagger at his attacker to buy time to rub a fist or fingers against his eyes. Finally he could make out a blurred image of the tall man. Cosmos leaned forward and sucked in his belly as the hazy figure swiped the spear at his belly, running at him. The back swing of the spear shaft caught him impossibly hard in the chest, throwing him off his feet.

The spear wielders laughed in an uproar as Cosmos flew backward then crashed to the ground in a small cloud of dust, grunting in pain as he finally rolled to a stop. "Wonderful!" he roared. "I have never fought against another berserker."

Berserkers were ancient warriors who fought with wild unrestrained aggression, always looking for another war. People thought they all died out when their number thinned, partly due to a fruit they unknowingly ate that made them sterile. Barren, infertile, they continued to fight battles until they were a passing memory. The otherworldly, ethereal energy you get from astral projection was said to have been learned from berserkers.

"A berserker!" Jane gasped.

"He can't deny it. I can feel the wraithlike energy surrounding him. He was holding me back from releasing my strength inhibitors. He is still trying to hold me back. But as you just saw, I now wield my full strength," his opponent said.

Cosmos was writhing on the ground in agony, like the proverbial worm on a hook. So this dark giant of a man claimed to be a berserker. That might explain the unprovoked constant pull toward rage. His vision was still hazy, but the new flow of tears was helping clear it. Cosmos could feel his lost sword under him, if he could just push the pain aside long enough to finish this.

"All that he's doing now is allowing me to keep a clear head, and it's wonderful!" the Berserker cheered.

"Berserker," Cosmos said through clenched teeth as he got up to his knees, sword and dagger in hand.

The berserker turned from Jane to look at Cosmos, flexing through the pain.

"I am going to bleed you!" he taunted like before, dragging blades over each other making the scraping metal sounds again. Last time he taunted him, the berserker declared he would hit Cosmos like a landslide. Letting out a wheezy breath, Cosmos didn't disagree with the comparison.

The berserker started to say something as he made his way toward Cosmos. But just then, Cosmos closed off his astral projection, putting a metaphysical container over it, like covering a dark blanket over a lamp, effectively shutting off the light. That made Cosmos less aware of his senses, dampening the pain he felt somewhat. But the berserker no longer had him to hold the balance for him; his eyes lost focus then seemed to promise pain and devastation to anyone who got in his way. And Cosmos was in his way—his one and only target. Suddenly he was charging Cosmos the people behind Cosmos scattered no longer standing near the border.

Cosmos was still filled to overflowing with energy. But Cosmos wouldn't have the precognitive abilities afforded him by the extrasensory perceptions of astral projection. Cosmos stood up and entered the whirling defense stance. Each attack was staggering. He dared not let any hit him. His hands were ringing from the force of the blows. The berserker was an inferior fighter compared to Cosmos, but his strength was paranormal. And he had Cosmos retreating, dexterously dodging more attacks than he was blocking because his hands were hurting. From the barrage of merciless attacks, the onslaught went both ways. But the berserker wasn't of a mind to block or even care if he got killed.

"It is over. He is beaten," Cosmos said, still retreating. Finally he was able to nick his neck. "Captain, you need to restrain him unless it is ok for me to kill him now."

"Why did you not just keep holding his sanity a little longer until you could beat him?" Captain Sanders demanded, obviously perplexed at how to put a stop to the rampage of their berserker.

"Jane, will you please take over before I have to take his head off just get his attention for a bit or something?" The dagger was knocked out of Cosmos's hand. He didn't spare it a glance, just took the sword in both hands and continued to defend himself.

"Sure, I would be glad to beat some sense into the senseless," Jane said, running to intercept the mad man without even drawing weapons. The berserker didn't spare her a glance until she was within range of his spear. Cosmos blocked it so he couldn't bring it against her. She jumped feet first at him, scissoring his legs with hers. That forced him to fall down hard and fast face first into the dusty ground. When he stood, Cosmos was glad to see Jane was his primary target.

Cosmos smiled as the crowd took a collective breath when the berserker went after Jane. She did two backhand springs, drawing him away from Cosmos, then ran and leaped at him, kicking the berserker three times in the chest. He staggered then fell on his back this time. Then the crowd let out the collective breath, deciding she could handle him herself.

Cosmos nonchalantly started gathering his discarded daggers. He had to laugh when Jane swept the feet out from under the Berserker, knocking him down for the third time. He knew what the onlookers didn't—if she'd use her weapons on him, she would kill him. Now she had a hold of the opposite side of his spear. He tried to jerk it away from her, but she jumped at him, using the force of the pull to propel her feet even harder into his chest. The berserker was the one forced to let go of the spear. They both fell to the ground. This time, there was a roar of cheers from all those gathered.

"Well, I am ready to kill him unless you have a plan to bring him to sanity," Jane said, beating each of the Berserkers legs with the less harmful end of the spear, then ramming it into his chest to slow his advance more. He staggered but didn't stop.

"I do not think he has an aura around him. He does not astral project..." Cosmos tried to explain how it felt. "He was leeching off me like some sort of parasite, a sponge incapable of independently balancing himself."

"I know you are leading somewhere with this line of reasoning, but just tell me what you want me to do." Jane dodge to one side then swept the berserker's feet out from under him again with his spear.

"Astral project, he should get some level of balance from the two of us. If not, then we can leave him to them. He really is not our problem. If he cannot control himself and they cannot control him, then he should have died a long time ago." Cosmos was shaking his head sadly at the poor Berserker as Jane spilled him to the ground again.

"There...yes, he is leeching, pulling hard with rage of course." Jane was moving smoother, even more grace-fully than normal, and that was saying something. No one else would notice, but Cosmos knew it meant she was astral projecting.

"Letting him leech will not be enough at this point. He has too much rage. You must burn it away, consume it." Cosmos was astral projecting now too; he could feel the familiar ethereal presence of Jane, her wraith-like aura. He knew feeling her phantom was because she was projecting, but he guessed that because they were twins, they had a sort of symbiotic relationship. Cosmos couldn't understand why a berserker wouldn't have an aura. But he could feel him pulling him toward rage again. "You know how to forgive and forget. That is like what we are trying to do. Forgive him his rage, then forget it—burn it away, so it is not even a distant memory. And think of a clean flame when you do it. Do not let it burn black. We don't even want any smoke to be left of his rage."

The berserker started attacking more smoothly, gracefully, unlike the mad bull or some rabid animal. That he had seemed when Jane was knocking him down over and over again. He was smiling now and block-ing almost every attack against him, enjoying himself. His facial expression was a mirror image to Jane's now bliss; he was in harmony. Cosmos decided it was time to stop astral projecting now. If the berserker couldn't stop with this little rage, then they would leave him to be put down like a rabid dog. Just before he quit, he felt Jane close off her astral projection. Without them, the berserker suddenly looked alone sad.

"Am I the loser?" the berserker asked, coming to a stop. He put a hand against his neck and found some dust-covered blood. "Oh yes, I remember now." Then looking at Jane, he said, "You didn't have to humiliate me." He looked down and started brushing dust off himself.

"It is not our fault you could not control yourself," she replied, picking up a couple daggers and handing them to Cosmos.

"Well, I haven't had a berserker to teach me, like you two obviously have," he said defensively.

"We are not berserkers. We are Sorrows. I am Jane, and this is my brother, Cosmos Sorrow. Surely you could understand we are much different, and just look at us, we don't have a drop of your blood in us."

Cosmos watched Jane reason with him. Finally the Berserker nodded resignedly. The two of them were average in every aspect; by all accounts, berserkers were always giants among men.

Now that the first part of the contest was over, Jane went to Captain Sanders, who seemed to have already relinquished command to her. She made subjection of him and asked things to be done, and he acted as commanded. Most of the gathered spear wielders were sent to the city to guard rooftops and to watch the night sky. She intended to find out where the abductors' base of operations was and attack it. Apparently, she had six of their gliding-demon costumes from the six that attacked her group. And if they don't catch some of them soon, she would have more made. They would start trying to follow them out of the city dressed like them, if need be. That got some people scared; they didn't like the idea of gliding over rooftops. The captain had some of the few soldiers who were still around to go get torches for his and Jane's contest because it was getting dark.

When he thought no one but Jane could hear him, the captain said, "Could you at least draw your weapons when you fight me? I don't want to be humiliated like what you did to Turlock, Jane Sorrow, please. Truth be told, I'm sure he was a better combatant than I will be. After all, I'm not a berserker."

"Neither are we," Jane said with a hint of anger at what he might be suggesting. He emphasized her name then went on to imply that she was a berserker.

Cosmos didn't like Jerald from the first time he saw him, upbraiding the soldiers for his failings as their commander. Now he was on the verge of blackmailing Jane if she didn't make her fight against him look challenging. Being labeled as a berserker would be a bad thing. Half the scary stories children tell were about rampaging berserkers, and parents tell them to their children to keep them under control. "If you don't watch that temper, it'll drive you mad as a rabid dog, just like a berserker." Whether Turlock believed he and Jane were berserkers or not, he dropped it. Cosmos was sure Turlock would have trouble just getting a drink at a tavern. People would know what he was and would fear some simple thing would set him off. So they refused service to save property damage and, maybe, people's lives.

Cosmos ignored their conversation. He and Jane had nothing to fear from the captain. They weren't berserkers, and he could always reprimand him later if he tried selling that story. Instead, he let his mind wander to Moyra, a much more pleasant subject than blackmail.

Moyra Sublime, her milk-white skin, blood-red hair, and fiery emerald green eyes, and just think she is here in the city less than a mile away right now, Cosmos thought.

It was easy to remember the defined line of her amazing long legs. That contagious smile—she could smile for any reason, and no matter his mood, he couldn't help smiling back. And best of all, she was exciting, fun, and competitive, whether it was swimming across a lake just to see who was faster or going hunting. How many girls enjoy those things? Her father called her Daughter of the Sand. What was the meaning of that? It could be a title. He knew they often gave people titles in the south, depending on their skill with astral perception and dream walking. She was a delightful enigma; someone he never had any disappointment in.

Jane and Jerald entered the dueling area from opposing sides; she came to a stop near the center. But Jerald rushed forward to attack, trying to force her to do something impressive. She sprinted back, stepping just as fast, so his storm of attacks hit only air. Just when he thought she was going to keep avoiding him, she dashed forward with weapons in hand. Her combination of vigor, daring, and style easily thwarted his attacks. He sidestepped, spinning his spear overhead, brought it down to stop hard against his shoulder, then twisted his body around, leveraging the spear around faster as he went. The extra speed surprised her. The mechanical advantage gained by using leverage increased the power of the hit too. She braced for it, but the physical force of the swing drove her back, feet sliding in the dust. She rushed him again, and he repeated the move. This time, she rolled under it and did a backhand spring before he could bring it to bear on her again.

Cosmos cheered, glad she wasn't going to let repetitive techniques trip her up. When she first bared her blades, he had been surprised because her sword was a reflective dark blue, almost black. It looked like it was lacquered or painted then polished. Last time he saw it, both her blades were like his, not even polished, let alone lacquered. The few soldiers gathered must have decided they were supposed to root for their captain because they started to provide support actively in favor of him with cheers, shouts, or applause whenever he attacked strongly or dodged one from her.

Cosmos cringed when Jerald stuck his hand in a pouch he was sure had blinding powder. But Jane saw it too and stabbed that hand with her sword, whirled in closer, and slashed his neck with her dagger, ending the duel.

Jerald cursed and raved loud, irrational, and incoherent at Jane for stabbing his hand. His powder pouch on his belt had a little blood coming out, along with a constant stream of yellow blinding powder.

Cosmos smiled, remembering how bad it stung to have that stuff in his eyes. *Serves you right! I wish I had done that to Turlock when he threw that powder in my eyes* he thought.

Jerald took his glove off; it looked like his hand would be okay. The blade had been turned the same way as the hand, so it went in between the bones, not severing them. The cut on his neck was bleeding just as bad. Jane hadn't been as careful as Cosmos was. But Jerald's armor had high flanges to guard his neck, so it was harder to get to.

Cosmos walked over to them, intending on telling Jane he was off to Brunswick to see Moyra.

"Well, my spear is yours. What's your first command as commander of the abductor countermeasure?" Jerald asked Jane as he handed her his spear.

She didn't take it, just looked at it. "You do not have to give away your spear. It is just a metaphor, a symbolism for passing partial command to me," Jane said, but Jerald offered it again, indicating he wanted her to take it. She did, but when he dropped his hand, she passed it to Cosmos. Jerald let out a low growl when Jane dispassionately passed on his spear. Cosmos kept his face indifferent, but he smiled inwardly, knowing Jerald thought Jane was being dishonorable. He also knew Jane would think Jerald was sentimental and silly for making anything of it. After his growl of displeasure, Jerald let it go obviously feeling it was his fault for pushing her to take it.

Cosmos didn't blame Jerald for feeling put off; the craftsmanship that was put into this spear showed a great deal of skill and expertise. Jane simply giving it away showed she thought little of the wielder and weapon alike. The only things on the spear he would change would be to put a thinner shaft on it that could flex, like the one on Turlock's spear, allowing it to move faster, and to add some tassels just under the spear point to quiet it as it sweeps through the air. If not for the whoosh of rushing air, it would have surely hit Cosmos when he was staggering blind. It would match the effect of short tassels that a hunter sometimes put on his/her bowstring, quieting the twang after the release.

"I want maps of the city, one of them marking all the buildings the abductors have taken people from."

Jane acted like she had already forgotten the spear of command.

"Yes, of course, right away...if you would like to go to an inn, I will have everything brought to you." Jerald said, turning to leave.

"You said the Dueling Bard, right?"

Jane nodded her head, but Jerald couldn't see with his back turned. Cosmos said yes so he could hear, then turned to Jane, tapping the spear shaft against her sword scabbard.

"What happened to your sword? Did you kill some blue-blooded noble and get it stained blue?" Cosmos said, laughing. "I cannot believe you had it lacquered. That is as silly as those people that fight with blades made of silver."

"No, it is a new kind of forging, a new kind of metal alloy. Look at it for yourself. Oh, and those people that fight with blades made of silver sometimes do that to counter a very real danger werewolves." Jane pulled the blade from her scabbard. The first job Jane was given upon her return from the south was to assassinate the Waif of Chance Harbor, a rumored werewolf.

Cosmos let the spear lean against his neck and took the sword from her. It was lightweight. He scratched a fingernail against it then bent it from side to side. Trying to break the lacquer, he slapped the flat of the blade against the sole of his boot. Holding it over a torch, it didn't smoke, so there was no paint, lacquer, or polish to burn away. Satisfied it was some new sort of steel, he tested the balance and gave it a few test swings.

"It is deceptively lightweight, harder to see in the dark, but best of all, it is harder than other blades. I have not had it long, but the edge is still as good as new, I doubt that I will have to sharpen it for some time."

They walked to her black horse. Cosmos laughed at Jane when she told him she named it Alabaster. Very bizarre, she has a twisted sense of humor; he never saw alabaster that was not as white as ivory. Yet she named a black horse *Alabaster* instead of *Ebony*, *Obsidian*, or *Midnight*. She countered that his horse, Eclipse, was white, but when there was an eclipse it would get dark. He nodded but thought about the white outline around the moon during an eclipse. He realized then when she mentioned his horse, Eclipse, that Moyra might think it insulting, wounding, or discourteous for him to give her gift back, so he decided to give her Cayenne, instead of the other way around. Besides, he liked the high-spirited young steed, and it felt good to have something from her.

"Do you know why Moyra gave Eclipse to me?" Cosmos asked. "It feels portentous or fateful."

She smiled, ducked her chin, and turned her head away, trying to conceal her amusement as they rode back to the city. "Do not say it is portentous. That makes it sound ominous or ill-fated. Think of it as auspicious, positive, and thank your lucky stars," Jane replied, making the last a jest.

Cosmos didn't appreciate her banter. "You are having entirely too much fun with this. That doesn't levitate my fears in the least. When a woman says something is marked by lucky signs or good omens, and therefore by the promise of success or happiness, it usually means a man is getting stapled down or at the very least becoming the brunt of a bad joke." No, it wasn't raising his fears from his shoulders, he felt like an oxen yoke was dropped over them.

They rode in silence until they were through the Brunswick city gates; Cosmos was glad that if any woman was trying to tie him down, at least it was Moyra.

"Forgive my little jest," Jane started to say more but got distracted by a group of revelers as they made their way through the city.

Cosmos had forgotten that tonight was the first night of the Festival of Seven. The noisy celebration grew into an uproarious party; kegs of spiced mead and ale sat in the road at a wide turnaround, where revelers were having an enjoyable time in the company of others.

"You take pleasure…enjoy party!" a stout drunken woman said to Cosmos, almost too slurred to understand. Cayenne came up to his side and pushed the intoxicated woman aside with her head. Cosmos laughed and then scratched the mare's mane and ears affectionately.

A short time later, they were putting their horses in a stable at the Dueling Bard Inn. Moyra came into the stable, beaming a broad smile of happiness and satisfaction. Cosmos couldn't ever help but smile when he saw her smiling; it was contagious. He could feel a glowing in his chest, which spread throughout his entire body. She was wearing a short white pleated dress that looked like she had grown out of it a few years prior. It would not matter if she were in a potato sack made from coarse hemp, burlap, or jute sacking. As they say, beauty is in the eye of the beholder—nothing could detract from her beauty in his eyes.

THE DUELING
BARD INN

The Dueling Bard Inn was built from red rectangular stone stacked tight and melded together craftily. It was three levels high, but only the bottom floor had high ceilings, allowing the common room to stay cool. The common room was large and wide without inner walls, except for one to close off the kitchen. To hold the weight of the upper floors, there were large redwood pillars here and there. The pillars were so wide it would take two men to reach all the way around one. They narrowed as they went up in the third-floor rooms, where one man could easily reach around one of them. The whole inn was decorated with red inside and out—red rugs with white fringe, red tented windows, and red canvas wall hangings, red candles in red translucent glass containers on the white common-room dining tables.

Patronage was good at the Dueling Bard, with rooms being let to travelers all the time and one family staying full time on account of their home having been burned down during a lightning storm, so they stayed there while they built a new one. Moyra met them, a nice family, husband and wife with three young boys.

The common room was crowded with many people; all the warm bodies made it uncomfortably warm inside. Moyra knew it would be hotter still outside. She missed her desert home, where you could be assured a cool night no matter how hot the day. But at least the days weren't nearly as hot here as in the desert. All sand and sandstones were attractive in its own way but gave little shade.

At the wall across from the stairs going up to the rooms, there was an empty fireplace. The fireplace sat on a raised portion of the floor, this area was being used for a stage. On the stage, there were entertainers— one man playing a lute, another trying to follow the tune with a flute, and a singer. The innkeeper, Mistress Ileana, was a tall heavyset woman, who boldly took a place in between them. She was singing beautifully and was no doubt the attraction that pulled so many people to her common room. Moyra guessed there were five times as many people crowded into the common room as there were rooms for. Mistress Ileana would make a good deal of money selling mead and wine to the crowd tonight.

In a space near the stage that was cleared of tables, people danced Moyra danced with Echo laughing. She wished she had a more suitable dress for the dance. She had long since forgotten about the competition with Bella. Otherwise, she wouldn't have been so comfortable and at ease. She liked the feel of him leading her securely across the floor. The only way she could be more contented would be if it were Cosmos's arms she were in. They agilely moved around each other able to move quickly and with suppleness, skill, and control. Echo moved with more fluidity than Gabriel did when she danced with him. Moyra thought that some of Echo's grace and litheness must come from combat training with Jane. She laughed happily as he spun her to the end of his arm then back in. Their dance consisted mostly of turns and half twists, which made her pleated white dress spread wide.

Moyra enjoyed dancing the way Jane enjoys dueling; fast and upbeat, it was invigorating. She felt sorry for Jane as she doubted Jane would allow someone to control her this completely. Moyra wondered how they could be so opposite and maintain such a good friendship. Where Moyra was at ease, Jane would be on edge. Moyra pulled her attention back to her dance partner for the end of the song. Echo spun her toward a table were they sat and watched other people start dancing to a new song.

"Do Jane and her brother get along well? I know they are twins, but even the closest of siblings can grow apart." Echo said while he messed with a candle on their table. His constant meddling made him seem younger to Moyra.

Why can't he find a nice girl a few years younger than him? Like all the other guys do, she thought. "Cosmos and Jane get along well enough, I guess. I don't know any of their other family. They are all part of the guild of mercenaries in one way or another. I first met Jane a few years ago. My father hired her to be my minder, or bodyguard as she called it, but I didn't meet Cosmos until recently."

Moyra's father had reason to believe she was in danger and wanted her to have a minder who could always be close at hand. Women who were competent guards were few and far between in the desert. Jane was more than adequate; she was better trained and had a stronger wraith than any of the other guards.

"You like Cosmos the way I like Jane. Can you truly say you would feel differently if he were a few years younger than you?" Echo asked as he pulled a dried imprint of red wax off his hand.

Moyra thought about it for a moment then shook her head conceding his point. "You're right in part, I guess. Married couples are often many years apart in age, but younger people seldom date older. If Cosmos were several years younger than me, I don't think I would acknowledge his pursuits until he was older. You understand, don't you? It's because he would be impressionable—ready to accept, open and easy, to be molded by the experiences, opinions, or personality of myself." Moyra felt that she finally got through to Echo because he nodded his head slightly in acceptance of her argument.

"Can I offer the two of you anything to eat and drink?" a serving girl asked, smiling warmly. She had on a red dress, keeping with the inn's décor, but her apron was white.

"A meat pie and a mug of mead will be all for me, thank you," Echo said as he fumbled one hand in his money pouch because he had red wax all over the other hand. Moyra laughed at him and replied that she had already eaten but that some water would be nice. The waitress said they were out of pie but offered him some soup instead, and he consented.

Moyra wandered to the common room, avoiding any more dances and wondering when Jane and Cosmos would be back. Moyra and Bella's little game of who would weave a better web of enchantment over the boys was a tie. Gabriel and Echo chose to dance with Moyra, but Caleb and Gemini danced with Bella. Mephitis and Avilla agreed that they were equals in captivating men. Bella brought rumors of regular abductions throughout Brunswick, which made Moyra dread the time she would spend here. Avilla told her that Cosmos and Jane had already been dueling outside the city.

Ha! Jane always pulls other people into her conflicts, Moyra thought smugly. Avilla couldn't stay to watch Jane's duel, but she talked constantly of Cosmos fighting a berserker. Moyra cursed Cosmos, mentally chiding him for being so careful against a foe who obviously intended to kill him. Moyra knew that the man he fought couldn't have had much berserker blood in him. It had been hundreds of years since any real berserkers truly roamed the lands. But their blood still plagued people across the realms. Moyra met an elderly couple in the desert once who had some berserker blood in them. Even in their old age, they argued and raged about the smallest things. It was said that the woman killed her husband in a raging stupor. Moyra thought it sad but probably for the best that the ancient warriors' blood was thinning out. Avilla also said that she joined the Spearwielder Guard with Gabriel, Caleb, and her brother Gemini.

Finally Moyra decided to go outside into the stables. Maybe a cool breeze would make it as cool outside as in. Besides, it couldn't possibly be as noisy and crowded out there, she resolved. She opened the door to the stable and couldn't help smiling with glee when she saw Cosmos. He was climbing down off Eclipse, the high-spirited young white steed she had given him as a gift of engagement. She hadn't been sure he knew it was an engagement gift, but she thought he knew seeing how uneasy it made him.

Moyra was sure beyond doubt now because he had a beautiful red mare with him she was sure was for her. When he saw her, she walked into the stables and was pleased to see him smiling warmly. *I guess he got over whatever reservations he had about us getting married,* she thought happily. She put her arms around him and kissed him deeply. He wasn't much taller than her, so she didn't have to raise much on her toes to look him in the eyes. Moyra pressed her forehead against, his separating their lips. When their heads came apart, he came in for another kiss, but she pulled away with a teasing smile. Then she kissed him lightly, coaxing him, in only to move away again. She laughed lightly with mocking satisfaction at having aroused hope, curiosity, and especially physical desire in Cosmos. She was distracted from her game with Cosmos as Jane loudly cleared her throat.

"Hello, Jane, I trust you won your duel after taking care of the berserker that was apparently too difficult for Cosmos," Moyra said to Jane but made it sound like a scathingly critical comment for Cosmos. She noted him wince in pain, involuntarily moving away as she slid her hands down his chest. *Blasted berserker*, Moyra thought, knowing full well his duel was why he was in so much pain.

"Howdy, Moyra," Jane said, pulling the saddle off her black horse named Alabaster.

Isn't that an oxymoron? Moyra thought.

Jane continued. "I am truly surprised there is enough berserker blood in people for them to be called berserkers anymore. You should see this Turlock. He looks just like the bards describe berserkers of old. A giant of a man with the strength of an ox, I would not have been surprised if Cosmos had not gotten up after the blow he received."

"I was about to ask Jane if I could borrow her saddle to go riding with you. But if you're too sore, we can go tomorrow instead. It's not every day you get thumped by a giant," Moyra said seriously, except for the last. She exaggerated *giant*, embellishing it with her doubt.

Cosmos was looking from Eclipse to the red mare and back again, about to say something, but Jane interrupted, "Yes, take my saddle. You better go for your ride tonight because I am going to have him teaching some of the Spearwielder Guard how to fight tomorrow, so he will likely be a more tender next time you get the chance to go riding."

"What? Teaching has always been your thing. Why can't I play with those glider things you talked about?"

Cosmos asked, looking affronted that she wanted him to play weapon master to a bunch of spear-wielding army brats. "Besides, we may need to know how to glide if we are going to find out where the abductors are taking people. Who knows what heights they ascend to soaring around like daft albatross away from the sea?"

"I was hoping Moyra would figure those out for us. She has always been more comfortable around heights than is sensible," Jane said, shaking her head, probably in memory of one of the many times they went climbing together.

Jane described the large cloth wings with rib-like supports going through them that the abductors used to kidnap people with. Moyra smiled broadly in suspense, feeling a flutter in her chest. She was eager at the possibility of escalating through the air like an eagle. Cosmos turned to her, smiling so wide he bared teeth and gums. They were obviously both dreamily thinking of the same thing.

Jane stomped her foot and shook her head angrily, growling, "You cannot both spend the whole day playing with oversized kites! We have a lot to do if we are going to end the threat to this city, and I cannot do it all by myself!"

Cosmos laughed. Taking Moyra's hand, he put on a meek expression, not hiding the amusement in his eyes. "Very well, Moyra can glide, soaring where eagles dare, and I will take my lowly place on the ground training spear wielders. But don't expect them to become the paragon warriors they all proclaimed themselves to be."

"You want to go change into something more comfortable, Cosmos? I want to talk to Moyra, and she still has to saddle Cayenne," Jane said.

Cosmos gave her a suspicious look that said he was apprehensive about what they might talk about. Moyra laughed at his hesitation; his suspicious nature was one of the few things she didn't like about him. But she realized she didn't dislike it, either.

"Aye, sure I need to wash this blinding powder out of my eyes anyway," Cosmos said.

Moyra sighed watching him go. She hated watching him depart; he seemed unattainable, and it made her feel weak.

"I am glad to see you have got it as bad as he does, but I doubt this infatuation will do either of you any good," Jane intoned as she put Alabaster's saddle on Cayenne. The name *Cayenne* fit the mare's color perfectly, but naming something after the hot red pepper leads you to believe it was hot tempered. As Moyra stroked her hand down Cayenne's neck, she decided this mild-mannered mare was anything but hot tempered. In fact, the mare seemed too mild for as young as she was.

"I know you feel less than enthusiastic about us joining in marriage. You fear that this magnetism Cosmos and I have for each other is temporary. But as the saying goes, the turtle makes progress only when it sticks its neck out. I am sticking my neck out, straining for every step," Moyra said, feeling timorous and a bit frightened that maybe he wouldn't lower his defenses to allow her closer.

Curtis L. Gray

"You make him want to be a better man," Jane said, putting a hand on Moyra's shoulder reassuringly, alleviating anxiety. "I have known you for years, Moyra. I do not mean to be apprehensive. It is just that I am so close to him. He is my twin after all. It is hard to be complacent when I feel him softening." Jane had a look of genuine confusion; she crossed her arms under her breasts.

Moyra watched bewilderment play across Jane's face as she absently leaned against her black horse. Alabaster snorted and stepped away from the weight pressing on him. Moyra laughed as Jane stumbled in her moment of mystification and almost fell.

"Your uncertainty is understandable. Though I have known you for a long time, Cosmos and I are just getting to know each other."

"But you want to get to know him as husband and wife. Nothing short of that will be enough for either of you, will it?" Jane asked then shrugged her shoulders in acceptance.

"Commander Sorrow, we have brought the maps you asked for." A trio of the Spearwielder guard strutted off the back of a two-horse chariot. The two-wheeled vehicle wobbled slightly as their weight left it. They had several scrolls that were surely maps and a long leather case that likely held large detailed, more expansive maps.

"Good. We will look them over. I plan to have guards posted at likely places the abductors may come this very night."

They went into the Dueling Bard, following Jane, talking about the heights of buildings that had been violated so far and what parts of the city those buildings were in and for what reasons they were targeted.

Moyra finished getting Cayenne ready for her ride with Cosmos. Then she went inside looking for him, wondering what was holding him up. He was talking to Bella and Avilla. The sisters were wearing form-fitting dresses. They probably would have dragged him into a dance if he didn't have one of his arms full.

"Sorry, I took so long," said Cosmos. He was wearing a white long-sleeved shirt that seemed to shimmer as the red light played across it from the common-room candles in short, wide red translucent glass containers. He also had on soft gray linen pants that looked comfortable and elegant. "Mephitis has been to several inns but could not find a room. So I let her have mine for her and her husband. I will just camp out tonight," Cosmos said in answer to Moyra's questioning look at his bedroll in arm.

"That's nice of you. I'll let Bella and Avilla take my room, and I'll just bunk with Jane."

Cosmos kissed Moyra on the cheek. She blushed, becoming embarrassed more from the giggles of Bella and Avilla than from the kiss.

"I hope you don't mind, but I told Mephitis that you would."

Moyra took his free hand in hers for answer; she liked that he knew her that well.

Echo stepped in between Bella and Avilla with bedroll in hand and asked, "Do you mind If I campout with you? Jane has been teaching me astral projection, but my wraith is much steadier while I am sleeping. My concentration isn't good enough that I can use it for fighting yet. Will you call it out for me tonight? Then I will just maintain it until morning."

Moyra widened her eyes in surprise that Echo would ask Cosmos to essentially be his dream guide. In the desert back home, you would only ask a relative or very close friend to be a dream guide. She was sure they had never met, yet he was showing a tremendous amount of trust in Cosmos.

"Astral projection is much more common in the desert, Moyra," Cosmos said, squeezing her hand. "Here, it is learned the same way it has been since the ancient berserkers of old showed us how. There are very few of us that can learn it that way, only people with very strong auras. So there is no danger in asking for help. Indeed there are so few of us that we almost always have to learn from strangers."

Moyra relaxed. He was right; someone with a strong wraith had nothing to fear from being taught by a stranger. She shivered at the thought of being taught to dream-walk by a berserker. The nightmares you might conjure after feeling that murderous intent should be feared. But a strong wraith could easily force a far-stronger one out of their dreams even untrained.

"Gemini, Caleb, and Gabriel got beds in the servants' room at the top of a building down the street. Apparently, the servants were abducted. The owners were happy to have Spearwielder Guard protecting them, no matter how new of recruits they are," Echo said.

Moyra was sure Echo could have gotten a bed there too but suspected he hoped to learn more about Jane from her twin brother, Cosmos. Bella gasped, hearing that they would be staying in a room the abductors had taken people from.

"Bella, please don't tell Mom. She would freak out if she knew they might be endanger. It is unlikely they will return to a room they have already looted," Echo pleaded.

Moyra hated to think of people as spoils of war, but maybe that was exactly how the abductors viewed them.

"She won't tell, or I'll shave off her eyebrows in her sleep," Avilla said, elbowing Bella in her side playfully.

Bella's jaw dropped, and she put a hand to her eyebrows, a look of horror on her face. Moyra laughed and then cringed, feeling disgusted at the thought of being without eyebrows. She involuntarily raised her hand to her own eyebrows.

Cosmos laughed. "Sure, Echo, is it? You can camp out with me as long as you promise not to shave off my eyebrows in my sleep."

"It's not funny," Bella said defensively, crossing her arms under her breasts. Moyra elbowed Cosmos in the ribs, knowing he was making fun of her as much as Bella.

Echo set his bedroll down on a table, then jumped up to sit beside it, and then started playing with a cup of hot wax from a candle that had just now gone out.

"Well, if you do not want to go for that ride, I am going to get some sleep because Jane promised a trying day tomorrow," Cosmos said in a frustrated voice, as though the holdups were Moyra's fault. Moyra laughed, taking the jibe in stride, as she pulled Cosmos to the door so there would be no doubt that he was the one delaying.

As they rode out of the city, they were surprised to see how many people were still coming into Brunswick. Everyone wanted to enjoy the night dancing and celebrating the festivities, it seemed. Or maybe some were rushing in so that they wouldn't become prey to the abductors. Moyra made Cosmos promise not to camp too far away from the city and not to make a fire or anything that could draw the abductors' attention. He chided her for being silly and overcautious but otherwise agreed, if only for her peace of mind. She was astounded when he told her that Jane said they were taking as many as six people a night! Usually, less and sometimes, they wouldn't hear of anyone being taken for a week or two, only to find out that the abductors had taken a group of people from a wagon train during that time. Moyra wondered angrily how often abandoned wagons were taken by thieves and no one was ever reported missing!

"I have known very few people that could do astral projection while fighting. Most lose their concentration and cannot hold their aura of sensations, or wraith as Abdulla my teacher calls it. He was the only weapon master that could hold his in combat, or even had one, according to Jane. It felt much different than when Jane did it, weaker, thinner, and he didn't gain strength or speed from it. But he could sense a much wider area than we could. When I dream-walk, I can sense an area as far as the eye can see," Cosmos said.

Moyra was glad for the change of subject. Her thoughts had resided on abductors and abductions too much that evening. In the desert, everyone called astral projecting wraithing. Astral projection sounded okay if you were describing dream walking, but the skill was used at least as often awake as not. Wraithing was used for fighting and for scavenging for food bugs, small animals, plants, and most importantly water. Someone like Abdulla would be placed in a position of respectability, morally above reproach, in accordance with accepted standards of correctness or decency. Moyra decided that Abdulla's position as weapon master for a guild of mercenaries was satisfactory in these lands of plenty.

"There was another teacher or weapon master that could do astral projection. But his was different too. If you would call Jane's wraith red, then his was a mild blue. He said he could not use it for fighting, that it was like resting restoring his chakra, kind of like he was relaxing, lying down in the shade during the heat of the day. Jane never admitted to sensing his aura, or anyone else's, other than mine," said Cosmos, seeming perplexed at the many different types of wraiths.

"I am sure she would feel their wraiths if she approached them dream-walking. Here, everyone was trained like berserkers of old on how to release their wraiths. In the desert, people learned astral projection by sleeping, contemplating, or meditating under the stars," Moyra said, studying Cosmos. He was uncomfortable, even in pain, from his duel. She hoped he didn't have any broken ribs. "The type of wraithing you just now described is the most common. I think every wraith energizes, but we are ignorant of what all they can be used for."

They rode down to the west below Brunswick to the closest part of the Aroostook River. There was a large three-mast ship at the docks, with sailors preparing to go. It was named *Clytemnestra*. They came to a stop, not wanting to get very close to the water, because mosquitoes were swarming near the edge of the river. Cosmos grunted in pain his chest hitting his saddle as he climbed down from Eclipse.

"So what do you think of your new horse?" Cosmos asked as Moyra climbed down from Cayenne.

"There is not a mean bone in her body," Moyra said happily, although she was disappointed he didn't say something formal like she did when she gave Eclipse to him. He rubbed his hand up and down Cayenne's neck; it came to a rest on top of Moyra's.

"Moyra Sublime, I, Cosmos Sorrow, give you this horse, Cayenne"—he closed his fingers around hers— "hoping she will bring you safely wherever you go and selfishly hoping she will always bring you back to me."

Moyra smiled, putting her arms around Cosmos and resting her head against his neck. He put his hands around her and rested his head against hers. She could feel him flinch when one of her tears touched his neck. His proposal wasn't as elaborate or ornamented as hers had been. But he used both of their full names, and you couldn't expect much more from a man.

A dust devil swirled up the road, stirring Cosmos's soft white shirt and Moyra's hair. They walked away from the road, leaving the dock, ship, and noisy sailors behind. The horses followed, nibbling on clumps of grass and swatting at their sides with their tails.

After they had walked a ways, listening to the river and enjoying each other's company, Cosmos turned to Moyra and gave her a hug. "Moyra, let me feel your ethereal self, your wraith as you call it."

His words sounded distant, hungry, and hollow, at the end reverberating. She thought it must be because of the way he was taught to astral project. He was pushing emotion away, focusing on the moment, tensing like a bull preparing for impact. Moyra sighed relaxing, allowing him to hold her weight. Her eyes fluttered, and she almost slipped into unconsciousness—the part of the mind containing memories, thoughts, feelings, and ideas that she was not generally aware of but that manifest themselves in dreams and dissociated acts. Just this side of oblivion, Moyra felt Cosmos's wraith for the first time.

"The way we do it is as different as our wraiths are," Moyra said, as she marveled at how thick and tangible his aura was she could almost feel it against her skin. In a dissociated group of mental processes from the rest of her mind, losing their usual relationship with it, she could feel the pain in Cosmos's chest. Moyra couldn't fight while wraithing; it wasn't a question of concentration but empathy. She would feel every attack she inflicted against her foe. Moyra didn't mind not being able to use it like that because it didn't give her strength and speed like Jane and Cosmos get from theirs. Unlike Jane's, his was a welcoming ambiance, holding her wraith like he was holding her. Jane and Moyra's wraiths always pushed against each other almost to the point of being hostile. Moyra's wraith was so receptive to his it made her think of the morning glory flowers opening up to sunlight.

He sighed, relaxing just a little in Moyra's arms, which was strange to her because she was feeling more invigorated. "Yours is hungry, but it is not pulling on me like the berserker Turlock was. It is more like a great big lazy cat lying down, soaking up energy, revitalizing."

Moyra was taken aback by how similar their comparisons were.

"I know we cannot see auras, but I am sure yours is the same fiery emerald green as your eyes are," Cosmos said in awe.

Held tight in his arms, Moyra could feel his wraith feeding hers. It was like his wraith was trying to wake hers to bring it out to play in the world it knew so well. Cosmos relaxingly told Moyra that maybe hers was saying take it easy. There was a whole dreamy world to be explored on just the other side of oblivion.

"Yours isn't as dark as Jane's. It's a pale red or bright orange," Moyra replied, wondering if she should elaborate telling him how tangible his feels.

Cosmos laughed. "I never thought what color mine might be."

Moyra could remember Jane saying that her astral projection was green, but she had forgotten. Now hearing Cosmos elaborate on it so reverently made her smile. She was sure she would never forget the color of her wraith again.

"Something must be wrong," Cosmos said, sounding concerned. Moyra's apprehension grew when he stepped back, feeling his chest. "The pain is gone. It should be magnified while I am astral projecting." He closed off his wraith, while Moyra drew hers in like a breath of warm air at the same time. "It does not hurt now that I am not projecting either." He took a deep breath, apparently checking for pain in any of his ribs.

"This is going to sound strange, but I think my wraith healed you," said Moyra. She could remember feeling his pain when she was wraithing, and the pain was slowly going away as his wraith fed hers. "My wraith never gives me speed or strength, but I feel invigorated with both now. I think there was a sort of trade. Your wraith gave me what it normally gives you, and mine healed you. That must be why I heal so fast. It's my wraith's doing."

"Wow! I have never heard of healing by astral projection. It is not anymore extraordinary than some of the other things attributed to it though, I guess," Cosmos said sounding impressed.

"Now that the exchange is complete, how soon do you wish to proceed?" Moyra asked, kissing him deeply so that they were both breathless. Left in his hands, it was sure to be a short engagement. She was wondering if they would be married right away before the Festival of Seven ended three days from now. Men seemed to think the wait was only difficult for them. She was glad Jane would be there, but she didn't know anyone else in his family.

Moyra was saddened that her father couldn't stay for the wedding or even to find out if Cosmos would

Curtis L. Gray

to enslave you?" She could feel hot angry tears coming down her cheeks. Cayenne obediently trotted to where Moyra stood alone. Moyra mounted and rode away, angry at how such a promising evening turned around.

"Do not ride with your nose so high in the air, Daughter of the Sand! Your new mare may break her leg in a prairie dog hole," he said her title angrily at her for leaving without a better explanation. Her father had only called her that once where Cosmos could hear. He apparently picked up that it was a title and used it now to prod her. She couldn't bear to tell him Eclipse was intended as an engagement gift while feeling so much indignation from their misunderstanding. Tomorrow, her ire would die down and she would explain it to him.

When she returned to the Dueling Bard Inn, she instructed a stable man to take care of Cayenne. She wanted to be in her room before Cosmos got back so she wouldn't have to see him again tonight. She didn't rush back, but he would have to if he hoped to talk to her. Because of the way Eclipse reacted when she leaped away from Cosmos, he would probably have a little trouble getting the startled horse. The simplest course of action would be to just camp there and not even come back for Echo. The thought of Cosmos out there alone bothered her, so she resolved to tell Echo were he would camp. She also reminded him not to start a campfire so as not to attract unwanted attention. Something about that ship preparing to leave bothered her; it would be dangerous to sail at night. But that's obviously what they were going to do. The Aroostook River was wide and deep but deceptively fast, and it would be hard to see rocks and shore at night.

ON MIST-COVERED SHORES

Cosmos stood shirtless on the shores of the Aroostook River. A thin gray cloud of water droplets condensed in the atmosphere just above the river. The thin fog was cool, a welcome relief from the night heat. He had Eclipse's front legs hobbled loosely together with a rope to prevent the steed from running away in the night. Cosmos liked camping out; the mist would make it comfortable as long as it didn't get too thick and wet.

Cosmos sighed, remembering what Jane had said earlier that day. "It is good to see you again, Cosmos. I fear Moyra plans on asking you to go home to the desert with her. When she leaves, if you go south with her, it may be years before I see you again." So Jane had known fully well Moyra's intention on giving him her horse Eclipse. It had made him excited to think Moyra wanted him to go along with her, especially because the enigma known as Moyra Sublime that he couldn't get his mind off was the main reason Cosmos wanted to go south. The more he learned about her, the more questions he had. He felt as though an oxen yoke was being fitted for him. But was glad it was one of Moyra's making, so Cosmos resigned himself to try and think of it as auspicious, per Jane's advice. "Do not say it is portentous. That makes it sound ominous or ill fated. Think of it as auspicious, positive, and thank your lucky stars," Jane told him earlier that evening.

In the distance, the sound of an approaching horse could be heard. Cosmos wondered if it could be Moyra returning, and he felt the pang of regret and shame of having caused her tears. He had intended to make chase and apologize, but in her hasty escape, she spooked Eclipse. By the time he captured the horse, she would have been bolted behind her room door at the inn. The rider didn't have to come very close before he was sure it wasn't her, too tall and broad a man.

"Hey, Cosmos," Echo said companionably, "Jane was afraid you gave Moyra the white horse instead of Cayenne. She wanted me to make sure you knew Moyra meant it as an engagement gift."

"Engaged, huh? I did not know she used Eclipse for affiance. I never would have expected her to ask me in such a roundabout way. They do many things different on the sandy plains than we do here," Cosmos replied, feeling Echo's eyes measuring him "Not to worry, I gave her the red horse Cayenne. That's enough about that. If you are going to be any use to Jane, let's get you astral-projecting with a strong, invigorating aura. You said Jane has been teaching you, right? So I am guessing you don't have any trouble cutting it off or covering your projection. The fastest way for me to teach you to uncover it or reconnect is to summon your aura over and over. You just cover it back up every time you feel that you have a firm enough grasp on it to use for fighting."

"All right, I will be ready in a moment," Echo said as he unsaddled his horse and hobbled it near Eclipse.

"Draw your weapons and swing at me a few times before I beckon your inner image. It's no good if you always have to be relaxed before using it," Cosmos said while walking in the rising mist. It was getting thicker; he could no longer clearly see his bedroll that was near the saddle and supplies. The lamppost from the not-so-distant ship docks cast a mixture of red-and-yellow shade across the white mist.

Echo moved near Cosmos and drew his blades, and then he closed his eyes, obviously trying to concentrate on pushing away his emotions so that he could astral-project. Without a moment's hesitation, Cosmos stepped forward with his left foot and kicked Echo in the chest with his right, careful to use the flat boot sole rather than kick with the hard toe so as to knock off balance but cause no harm.

Echo fell on his back coughing, rolled to his side, and stood back up. "Sorry, what did I do wrong?" Echo asked, looking at Cosmos sheepishly.

"First off, you didn't swing at me like I told you to. Second, you closed your eyes. Embrace your senses that don't exclude sight. When a cobra sheds its skin, even the skin over its eyes peels off," Cosmos replied, then took a step back and nodded to Echo.

Cosmos contented himself parrying Echo's attacks, circumventing them without actually blocking. By the second attack, he was already astral-projecting as he continued to instruct Echo. His voice sounded hollow and distant to his own ears; in this state, he was confident. Confident that he could parry the novice Echo's half-hearted attacks more easily barehanded than with sword and dagger. Within a few minutes, Echo was astral-projecting too; instantly, his swordplay became crisper and much more precise. His wraith was stronger than expected, an ethereal presence just out of sight and hearing but made Cosmos's other senses tingle all the same.

Echo was pleasantly smiling to himself, pleased with his achievement when Cosmos told him to draw it back in and cover it so they could start over. Cosmos was glad that Echo had a strong invigorating aura, but it was more work getting him to summon it than he had hoped. Rather than being a wolf calling a cub out to play, it felt more like carrying it out of the den by the scruff of the neck. It took a dozen tries before Echo could astral-project in combat on his own and another dozen before he could consistently do it every time.

It was getting late, and the mist had worsened to the point that they could no longer see the horses in the deepening darkness unless a dock lamp was in the background.

"This time, focus your spirit with your projection as far as you can reach with attacks, no more or less." Cosmos swiped a dagger out in a straight arm feint as though he intended to throw it.

Echo flinched and stumbled.

"You see, I am well out of your territory, the space you can consider as your own. Imagine a protective bubble around you, and focus the projection to heavily fill it up but not expand beyond that area. We are seven paces apart, yet you easily fell for the ploy because your wraith is encompassing us both," said Cosmos. He disliked explaining but Echo was too new at this to learn with experience alone.

"But I can clearly feel your wraith around me," Echo argued, raising his hands palm up and tilting his head to one side in Jane's what gives pose, obviously wondering why it was okay for Cosmos, but not for him.

"I am projecting in two domes, one at melee range, the second in range of accurately being able to place daggers. I will project in a third bubble if I have a bow and arrows handy. You need to refine melee range before you expand, and even then, it's best to have a second bubble that you can fill without retracting from the first. Of course, your presence will not be as heavy or your awareness as precise. But it's essential to be aware of your immediate area," Cosmos explained.

"I understand your ethereal presence did feel more overbearing at close range. Your wraith is suppressing to the point it is surprising that the mist rises undisturbed around you. I once read that it was hard to breathe in the presence of a berserker." Echo smiled broadly and continued. "Gemini joked that berserker's stench was just so intense people must have held their breath, ha-ha. The book was about astral projection though. It had a lot on shared dreams and dream-walking."

Cosmos smiled lightly. "Well, stench and dream-walking aside, even the youngest, weakest untrained berserkers were to be feared. They fought with wild, unrestrained aggression defying reasonable under-standing. A frenzied twelve-year-old girl could snap a grown man's arm if she were a berserker. In their rage, they bypass the body's natural strength inhibitors. We can normally only use about 10 to 20 percent of our muscle strength. Our bodies restrain us as a self-preser-vation instinct from harm or injury," Cosmos said, tak-ing weapons in backhand position, then seating him-self on his hunches to look out over the mist-covered Aroostook River.

"About two years ago, there was a bad mud slide not far from here. It crushed a barn and covered about a quarter mile of highway. A man was able to save him-self and a child by tearing the door off the overturned carriage he had been driving and taking shelter inside along with the other passengers. Normally, he wouldn't have had the strength. Even still, he pulled one arm out of socket, and the other arm was not undamaged either. After battles, berserkers spent considerable time in agony from similar unintentionally self-inflicted harm," Cosmos said, turning his attention to Echo, who stood stretching his weapons in every direction to, presum-ably, gauge the area he would focus his astral projection.

"Does Jane project her astral presence in a second bubble like you do?" Echo asked inquisitively.

"No," Cosmos replied simply.

Echo came to face him directly weapons in sheaths, head tilted slightly to one side.

"I wear twenty-four daggers on my armor, not count-ing my off hand weapon. Normally, I wouldn't have used a second projection area while wielding only two weapons. I guess I may have unconsciously felt threatened because you were claiming so much space with your wraith. That and I never duel out of armor, so it has become a habit to astral-project in two areas," said Cosmos, surprised to see Echo so obviously giving his undivided attention like a child waiting for the best part of a story.

"Do you think Jane will project in a second area now that she has a boomerang?" Echo asked, sounding dejected that that was all there was to Cosmos's explanation.

Cosmos was bewildered, wondering what part of the conversation had snared Echo's attention. *Does Jane project her astral presence in a second bubble like you do?* Cosmos stood up, turned his back, and smirked. *So it is Jane,* he thought. He could hear Echo lightly curse and kick the dust under foot with little force. He decided to test the waters by talking about Jane a bit.

"She has honed her single combat skills armed and unarmed more than anyone I know," Cosmos said, walking to his horse, Eclipse. He placed his hand on the horse's neck and slid it down the foreleg, stopping just above the hoof. Slightly raising the hobbled hoof, he scraped the dirt loose with his opposite hand. "She tried daggers, net, spears, even a whip, and who knows what else. Jane may yet decide that a boomerang isn't to her liking, either. Women are fickle like that."

"Fickle? I don't mind that. I am often of two minds about various things. Jane is decisive when it counts," Echo said.

Yes, as long as she has a clear primary target, Cosmos thought.

"She said you are better at fighting a group of assailants than anyone she has ever known. I asked if you were better than her. She said, 'Not one on one but that a group of people that could best her nine out of ten times would lose by the same percentage against Cosmos.' Also that you would lose nine out of ten times against her but, if asked, would play it down to four out of five," Echo said, raising an eyebrow, as if waiting for confirmation or denial.

Cosmos decided not to disappoint. "Well, we each have our own opinion regarding that. And a group that could defeat her would probably have at least a 50 percent chance of defeating me too."

He began unrolling his bedding and glanced curiously at the dock as more lamps were added to compensate for the deepening mist. *They must be expecting a wagonload of supplies, passengers, or something else coming from the city*, Cosmos thought. He was surprised that they would sail at night but knew there were ways to navigate under harsher conditions. But even if they had a long-range astral projector, he or she would have to be dream-walking to know the ship's position in the river, and they would have to have a second person astral-projecting to communicate with the dreamer. Night and mist, combined with the ship's great size, would make travel very dangerous. But they could sail most the night before approaching any major bends in the river.

"I find fighting Jane troublesome, but she will fight me more vigorously than she would another opponent, maybe even in a life-and-death confrontation," Cosmos, said returning his attention to Echo, who looked doubtful as he took off his boots and prepared his own bedding.

"I could never find Jane troublesome," Echo said under his breath as he lay down. Then he adjusted uncomfortably because Cosmos laughed obnoxiously.

"Ha-ha, even Jane would object to that statement. She has said good-humoredly that her middle name is *Trouble*. Jane has an impetuous nature, acting on the spur of the moment without considering the consequences. That's part of her charm sure, but troublesome nonetheless." Cosmos was trying to lighten the blow of laughing at something he wasn't supposed to hear.

"Well, I guess the cats out of the bag. Do you know if Jane has someone she likes?" asked Echo.

"Uh…umm…well…umm…ha-ha…six days, you cannot have known her longer than that," Cosmos said. Jane had written him a letter saying she would be a merchant guard for a family that was bringing horses to Brunswick. The letter said she would arrive in six days from the southwest. Cosmos knew of a ranch about four days away and guessed it would take little longer with the wagons.

"Aye, well, my parents fell in love at first sight, or at least my dad did. Mom said he had to win her over. They were married less than three months later. There isn't a happier couple alive," Echo replied proudly.

Cosmos relaxed, closing his eyes and taking a deep moist breath. He remembered Jane saying that Terry had died during an attack a few weeks ago. Cosmos liked Echo, even though he only knew him a short time. "I thought she liked someone once. He was confident, charismatic, competitive—I don't like to speak ill of the dead—but kind of a snob. Sorry, but you should learn these things from her. She would be mad at me for saying unnecessary things," Cosmos said uncomfortably, realizing Jane and Moyra must have had similar conversations after he and Moyra first met. He heard Echo relax and begin breathing rhythmically asleep.

As Cosmos lay covered by mist not far from the Aroostook River, listening to the steady water flow, a cool breeze came across the river and up toward the city of Brunswick. The breeze also brought indistinct congratulatory shouts from the three-mast ship *Clytemnestra*. He also heard what sounded like a sheet or laundry blown by but strangely going the opposite direction the breeze would have taken it. As the sound was repeated, it reminded him of the kites he and his twin sister, Jane, used to fly when they were young and were still living at the guild hall. Suddenly he was wide awake and on alert—Jane had said the abductors had winged gliders like oversized kites. Did that mean they were attacking the ship? He reached a hand under his pillow and grasped his best dagger, the one that he used for an offhand weapon. It was about half the length of a small short sword, and its shape was not unlike that of a boomerang. This was appropriate, considering Moyra's boomerang-enthusiast father had given it to him. As Cosmos got up, he left his sword but took his pillow, which was actually his cloak.

"What's amiss?" Echo asked groggily. Still astral-projecting, that was probably the only reason Cosmos's faint movement had disturbed him.

"I am going to the ship. Jane taught you to dream-walk, yes?" Cosmos asked.

Dream-walking is the easiest astral projection skill to learn. You can literally do it while sleeping. Aside from placing an image of yourself in others dreams and having a minor control over their dreams, you can also perceive the area around you. Inanimate objects are the easiest to perceive, but a strong aura can find live beings. Nightmares are a very real danger to the dream-walker; that's why dream guides are essential. Nightmares are creatures of the dreamer's creation though, so new people seldom encounter them. The problem is that if they do encounter nightmares, it's unlikely they will know how to vanquish them.

"Yes, but there are no horses to keep track of. Lest they stray tonight, ours are hobbled—surely you didn't forget," Echo complained. Jane must have had him astral-project as he slept to help keep track of the horses on their journey to the city of Brunswick.

"Just keep track of me, then convey my findings to Jane or Moyra. Should be easy to find ether of them in the dream because they almost always astral-project while sleeping, and Jane has been teaching you," Cosmos said.

"Well, Jane angrily told me to stay out of her dreams after I saw her slay a werewolf in one. Jane said it was a person, and she was Annie, the Waif of Chance Harbor, Jane was sent to assassinate." Echo sounded hurt or ashamed Cosmos couldn't tell which. "Besides, the only other person's dream Jane guided me too was Moyra's, the last night of our trip to Brunswick. Moyra easily pushed me aside, causing me to lose my astral projection. I didn't know who Moyra was then. Jane just said her best friend was a little ways behind us and to try and find her. Later, Moyra accidentally called my wraith when she fell asleep in the wagon. I knew that she knew Jane, but it wasn't until then that I realized Moyra was the best friend," Echo explained lengthily.

Cosmos felt a flush of jealousy that Echo had felt Moyra's ethereal self before he had. He decided then to have Echo specifically look for Jane rather than Moyra. "Well then, just think of me when your projection gets to Jane's dream and she will let you in. Explain that the abductors are down here at the ship *Clytemnestra* and that I am gathering more facts."

Echo eagerly nodded, no longer showing any signs of drowsiness. Lethargy gone, Echo had to take a meditating pose in order to dream-walk through his enthusiasm—legs crossed, eyes closed, head down, and hands together, forming an overlapping circle with his thumbs crossed atop.

Cosmos darted toward the water, twisting his cloak around his left arm so that he might shield himself from poison darts with it. Then he ran along the shore toward the ship to hide under the dock. The mist was thicker down there, making it harder to see or be seen. At this range, it was easy to hear anything that went on up above. Cosmos was surprised not to hear a heated battle, but it would have been one sided. Jane said the groups were of six gliders; the crew of a ship this size could be nearly sixty. He started feeling silly that he had thought they came here, so he climbed a support for the dock. About two thirds of the ways up the support, he heard a casual conversation.

"They were waiting for us. We checked a dozen buildings before finding any without guards and high enough for us to still glide over the wall."

Cosmos couldn't see who was talking, but the content marked the speaker as an abductor.

"The attack on the guard tower was supposed to silence those who knew too much about us and make this easier. Not only did you lose half your number, but now we can't go anywhere unchallenged. We knew what countermeasures they were taking before they put them in place. Now they are no longer randomly putting guards on rooftops with longbows but concealing them inside the best target buildings," the speaker continued.

"I made the best choice I could with what we knew. He suspected that we weren't bats eating our prey, but sentient beings enslaving our captives. Even the pretense of the ship under repair would have been gone once he learned that the guards he sent down here never returned," replied someone who sounded older, speaking with a voice of authority.

Cosmos heard footsteps and imagined him pacing. Cosmos hadn't yet seen the masked gliders but was skeptical that they could be convincing disguises of giant bats. "Besides, the new defenses were made by members of the guild of mercenaries that arrived today. They would have been implemented regardless of last night's exploits. After that first group disappeared a few weeks ago, I thought we would be losing members every night. Apparently, they tried to abduct an encampment of mercenaries and met their end instead. Luckily for us, bands of mercenaries avoid cities with

Spearwielder Guard garrisons, or they would have brought to light our true nature weeks ago. I will see to it that you are promoted. Capturing six even after they have done this much to stop us is commendable," the older speaker said.

"Thank you. The ship is leaving with two hundred new slaves. We have lost less than a dozen men achieving that. Any way you look, this is victory," the first speaker said in conclusion.

Cosmos was surprised to hear how many had been taken. He had assumed they were only getting one or two at a time and that they came randomly not every night. Jane would be furious that they got six tonight, despite the fact she only had time to implement a few countermeasures.

After climbing back down, Cosmos began meditating under the shelter of the dock. He found a specter of Echo and conveyed what he had heard to the apparition.

"Very well I will convey that to Jane," replied the white wraithlike apparition of Echo, who couldn't seem to decide whether to have his projection sitting or standing. One moment, it would be sitting across from Cosmos, mirroring Echo's meditating pose; the next, it would be standing, looking down on him.

"I am returning to you to put on my armor and prepare for an assault on the dock when Jane gets the guards down here. Try to get a count on how many people are here before then. I think it's at least a group of six, but there may be many more, and I think they will likely try to return to the eastern cliff before dawn. If not, then they'll probably just take off their disguises and be indistinguishable from the many people that have arrived at Brunswick," Cosmos instructed Echo.

Watching as the ship sail away, Cosmos couldn't help but feel disheartened. He had expected to arrive at the end of a confrontation between the ship's crew, deckhands hostile to a much smaller group of six abductors. Contrary to his expectations, they were allies.

COUNTERATTACK

Moyra Sublime awoke to what she guessed was about four hours before dawn. She was surprised to find she was standing, with Jane Sorrow half-supporting her as she was shoved to a corner. She had a bundle in her arms that she thought must be clothes because the corner she was forced to had the privacy curtain standing in its frame. After Jane assured herself that Moyra would stand on her own, she dashed across the room. Moyra watched as Jane gathered her abandoned armor strewn across the floor. Looking down at the bundle for the first time, she realized it wasn't simple clothing but the old armor Jane used to wear. All Moyra had to say was, "Why?"

"Oh good, you're awake!" Jane said with a sigh. "I was beginning to think I would have to clothe you." She had a deprecating look plastered on her face, shaking her head in exasperation. "It's like I told you—Echo and Cosmos need our help! The abductors are at the docks!" Jane said the last like someone tired of repeating themselves but the validation wouldn't stick.

Moyra was sure this was the first she'd heard of it. "Why didn't you say so before?" Moyra asked. Getting dressed in Jane's old armor, Moyra felt like she'd only gotten a few moments' sleep. Glad for the short rest she had obtained in the wagon during the last of the journey to Brunswick, she applied the armor, wanting to ask more but afraid of what she may hear.

"Cosmos heard them glide overhead and went ahead while Echo contacted us," said Jane.

"Oh no! I hope he is okay. Wait, do you think they are after the *Clytemnestra*? That ship was preparing to depart earlier. Attacking a ship that size would be ambitious for thirty people, much more so for a group of six," said Moyra in a rush, wondering if Jane's confrontation was singular or if they always attacked in groups of six people; three or four groups of six could have met up at the docks she guessed. "I sure hope the ship has already made its departure," Moyra said, just as Jane interrupted.

"No, you don't, and yes, the *Clytemnestra* has set off, but not before receiving tonight's captives!" Jane corrected.

There were two loud bangs on the door. Moyra slipped back behind the privacy curtain, almost knocking over the curtain frame as she put on Jane's studded leather skirt. Jane was already dressed, so Moyra wasn't surprised to hear her open the door.

"Commander Sorrow, I failed. The two servants we were guarding insisted we stand guard in the hallway rather than the balcony. They argued they couldn't sleep in that small room with three strange men hovering over them."

As Moyra came out from behind the curtain, lacing the bracers of her borrowed gauntlets, she recognized the intruder as one of the men who brought Jane maps earlier that evening.

"Their comfort shouldn't have concerned you over their safety. I told you that building could be a prime target—the roof would be easier to land on than many they have dared so far. Not to mention, the proximity to the wall allows an expedient evacuation," Jane chided.

"I am sorry. Robert convinced Tomas and me that we would hear anything going on in the room," he defended. "But when we checked on them, they were already gone."

"You cannot feint ignorance. You know full well they use sleeping poison and that there would be no struggle to hear." Jane started rummaging in one of several large bundles she brought to the room earlier until she found an unstrung bow, a quiver full of arrows, and a string, all of which she promptly handed to Moyra. Sighing, she continued, though no longer reprimanding him. "According to a dream-walker who contacted me moments ago, they got six people tonight. So yours wasn't the only failure. Either other guards were no more vigilant than you or I misjudged the heights of buildings they could successfully glide over the wall from." With that, Jane rushed out the room and downstairs armed and armored, with Moyra and the unnamed spear wielder hot on her tail.

"Is that supposed to make me feel better that I'm not the only failure?" he asked heatedly, but the venom in his voice was played down because when they got to the stable, he rushed to help Jane as she saddled her horse, Alabaster.

"No, I suppose not," Jane said smiling over her saddle. "But they say there is some small measure of solace in revenge."

"Just lead the way!" he replied, grinning back. He ran to his waiting two-horse chariot. Only one of his comrades was waiting unlike the previous time Moyra had seen him when he brought the maps.

Moyra found an abandoned bridle in the straw and dirt, but she would have to ride bareback because she didn't yet have a saddle for her horse Cayenne. She put the bridle on while Jane was saddling Alabaster. Then she strung the bow and adjusted her arrows while waiting for Jane to finish getting ready. Moyra was glad for the bow. Jane said she was only fair at melee and hand-to-hand combat, but Moyra had some confidence in archery. Anxious and raring to go, she crouched down, reaching up and taking a handful of horse hair. Leaping and pulling, Moyra scrambled onto Cayenne's bare back.

Before Jane mounted, Moyra observed her retrieve a cylinder two hands in length from her saddle bag. Along its length, she glimpsed small darts fixed in place, and she felt a foreboding. Moyra had been brought up to believe that vengeance is not ours and that malicious actions taken in vengeance were self-deprecating. "I don't think stooping to their level is wise. Surely, those you have lost would be expressing their disapproval," Moyra said. Jane gave her a steady look that betrayed nothing.

As they rode through the city, Moyra was surprised yet again to see how many people rode mules—pleasure mules, gaited mules, and driving mules everywhere she looked. She remembered her father saying, Mules ride smoother, and they are more surefooted, but most people who ride horses instead just know them as being stubborn headed." In the desert, mostly just horses were used, but you could see camels more often than mules.

They were well on their way out of the city Brunswick before Jane replied, "Oh, stop looking so glum. Melancholic doesn't suit you, Moyra. Apparently, it is not only your smile that's contagious. When you feel miserable, I feel miserable. Fine, I promise to only use the sleeping poison. Can you think of a better way to capture any of them?"

Moyra was relieved, but the potential danger Cosmos and Echo were in kept her mood dour as they raced to their side.

"Honestly, if you can't even bring yourself to talk to me, then I'll tell Cosmos how impossible you are to wake up or that you talk in your sleep and—snore!" Jane joked.

"I do not!" Moyra flushed, then smiled at Jane, thankful. Jane smiled back warmly as if to say, "You're welcome." The temporary break from constant tension was indeed welcome. Cayenne slowed, feeling her rider relax. Moyra spurred her gently to keep up the pace. *Please be safe*, she silently pleaded.

"I will stop at the gate and gather what guards can be spared!" the spear wielder shouted. Jane nodded. "Where do we meet?" he asked earnestly.

Curtis L. Gray

"The docks, of course! Where else?" Jane asked sarcastically, tilting her head to one side.

Perhaps she thought she told him while he was asleep the same as me, Moyra thought ironically, remembering having woken on her feet.

They continued out of the city, Moyra taking the lead, guiding Jane toward Cosmos and Echo's campsite. There had been a mild fog ridding through Brunswick City, but as they neared the river, it became heavily dense. They had to slow for the horse's safety, lest they break a leg on an unknown obstacle. Moyra neared the area she believed Cosmos to be camping. Raising a leg over Cayenne's neck and pulling the reins of the neglected bridle, saddle not impending, she slid quickly forward off the horse, taking a few running steps as she landed to quiet and slow herself, bow in hand by the time she landed.

"Cosmos, Echo," Moyra whispered urgently for them as loud as she dare, nocking an arrow at the same time. She was surprised to find Jane suddenly in front of her, silently taking the lead.

"Here," came a familiar voice in reply after they moved closer to the Aroostook River and called a few more times. "What took you so long? I was about to return to the dock. If they had horses, they could have returned to the cliff and been halfway up by now," Cosmos said energetically.

Moyra was glad to hear his voice but was mentally reprimanding him for planning to confront an unknown enemy alone. With Moyra's limited perception, Jane had already moved beyond her sight.

"Well, Moyra sleeps like the dead, and this blanket of fog slowed us down considerably," replied Jane.

Just as Echo's horse loomed into view then, Moyra could make out Jane and Cosmos side by side, their raven hair being the most prominent features in the gloom. Echo was in a meditative trance, which he must have used to dream-walk to contact Jane, and was now most likely using astral perception to try and follow the abductors' movements whatever they may be. Lastly, Moyra noticed Eclipse hardly distinguishable in the murky darkness.

"Let's get moving. The spear wielders will likely charge their chariots directly down the dock. I have no doubt they can overpower the abductors with surprise and sheer numbers. But if we want to know where that boat is going, we will need to capture some of them alive," said Jane.

"Four of the abductors have gilded off the dock and gone into a building on the other side!" Echo exclaimed, awkwardly rising to his feet. He beamed at Jane wile rubbing the circulation back into his legs.

Moyra hugged Cosmos as soon as she reached him. He seemed surprised, and that reminded her that they didn't part on good terms. He kissed her forehead and hugged her back but turned his attention to Echo. Echo was half a head taller than Cosmos but seemed juvenile to him in comparison.

"There are still four people on the docks, and at least two of them have gliders. We should attack now that they are separated, don't you think?" Echo asked.

"It is problematic that they can escape the docks if we attack there. But if we go after the others, those on the docks could attack our backs," Jane replied, shaking her head in dismay.

"Then why not go intercept the chariots? Have one charge the docks, making a lot of ruckus. The others can wait at the building where those on the docks are sure to flee. If the four of us confront those in the building at that time, we will still have the element of surprise," Cosmos suggested.

Jane nodded, and that put everyone in action. Cosmos unhobbled his and Echo's horses, Echo put on his armor, and Jane and Moyra rushed to gather their horses. They rode single file back toward the gates faster than they had come down. Cosmos was in the lead, leaning forward beside his horse's neck, sometimes turning abruptly to avoid rocks, brush, or prairie dog holes. Once they got to the cobblestone road, Jane took the lead as the most visible on her black horse. It seemed strange to Moyra that on a starlit night, the black horse would be the most visible.

"When we confront them, expect the worst. Underestimating them is your own peril, jeopardizing the rest of us in turn," Jane said, adjusting her gaze to Echo the least experienced of them. He nodded soberly. Jane's eyes flickered to Moyra, who nodded briskly. When she turned to Cosmos, her twin nodded with her simultaneously, acknowledging each other as equals. Jane pulled her reins, halting them all; her horse snorted impatiently.

"Who goes there!" called an unfamiliar voice. Moyra realized Jane must have stopped them after hearing the chariots approach.

"It is us, the Sorrow mercenaries. Welcome, Captain Sanders, you're a pleasant surprise. I did not know you were at the gate," Jane greeted as a four-horse-drawn chariot came into view. Next came the chariot pulled by two horses they parted with at the gate and two guards on mules bringing up the rear.

"Why didn't you tell me you had a spy and a dreamwalker no less or that they were taking the captives to the docks? I could have kept that ship from sailing! Do you have any idea how many people they have ensnared?" Captain Sanders asked angrily, shaking a fist bandaged carefully.

"Two hundred," replied Cosmos accusingly.

Captain Sanders looked genuinely surprised; apparently, his idea was far short of that number. Moyra was surprised too, but according to the rumors this had been going on for over a month. If they took six people most nights, then it added up.

"I only learned these things tonight. More importantly, we need to attack and capture them before they escape," Jane explained, giving Cosmos a look of disapproval.

The captain volunteered his chariot to be the one to charge the docks, partially because he expected them to stay and fight rather than escape. Moyra was surprised the guard captain expected the abductors to act like warriors and not the sneaky underhanded kidnappers they were. Sure they use force but mostly deception; the few confrontations seemed powerless, excluding the nature of their poisons. The second chariot would go with them, and one rider would go with each group.

Moyra was worried that they were taking too long and that the abductors would regroup before they set their plan in motion. As they approached the building, paper lanterns could be seen. Moyra hoped that meant the group was still split in two and the lanterns where there to guide their safe landing.

Jane instructed the guards to prepare an ambush hostile to the abductors' imminent landing. "Stay low, out of the light, and silent. When you engage them strafe left and right, they can only blow poison darts where their noses are pointed."

"Let's get inside" Cosmos said after moving to the building and slightly opening the door. He held the long curved kukris dagger in his left-hand and two smaller daggers in his right hand for easy throwing rather than his sword.

The building was long and squat with a rust-colored tile roof; the stone walls of the building were made from an assortment rocks, the lower half long heavy rectangular stones, the upper part mostly smaller tumbled river rocks.

"I will take point," Jane said, moving through the door ahead of them.

The first room had many sacks filled with lumpy items and crates of various sizes. Along the west wall, there were collapsed shelves loaded beyond capacity. From there was a jumble of items sloped inward toward their narrow path. The east wall had three closets with missing doors. The first was filled with old, dusty spears and muddy boots with cobwebs across their open tops. The second had rusty armor and two small crates stacked one on the other with a fresh, new scroll looking out of place on top. Moyra snatched up the small scroll and, upon realizing she didn't bring a belt pouch, forced it in an empty dagger sheath on her hip.

"*Oh!*" exclaimed Echo, jumping away from the third closet in surprise.

Cosmos let fly the two daggers in his right hand, then promptly clamped it over Echo's mouth. Holding Echo's head secured against his chest, he pointed into the closet with his left-hand dagger.

Curious Moyra peeked inside. At first, all she saw were three large sacks forced into the opening. *They must have been in the pathway before.* As her gaze rose up, there were several poles behind the sacks. On the ends of them were decapitated giant fox heads each with a bristly red mane. Two of the three wobbled in place, with daggers in them. On a fourth pole was a rusty helmet.

As Cosmos retrieved his daggers, Moyra realized they were all just helmets, but those three were a part of the abductors' disguises. Knowing they disguised themselves as bats, she remembered a book depicting fruit bats and decided they were frighteningly similar. *Seeing this, it is easy to imagine them eating their captives*, she thought, remembering Jane had said the night before that the city guards still had thought the abductors were animals.

Jane, who had been about to go through the next door, came back to see what had caused all the commotion. "This is good for us," she said, pointing a thumb over her shoulder at the disguises. "Their darts shoot from the masks, so only one of them is still armed with poison, but don't let your guard down."

"Echo, start astral-projecting. Your swordplay is still too sloppy. You will be a liability otherwise," said Cosmos.

Echo closed his eyes and had a look of concentration. Jane thumped his ear, and his eyes snapped open. "Right, sorry, shedding skin, even the eyes, just like reptiles do," he said apologetically.

Moyra wondered what he was talking about but decided now was neither the time or the place to ask. Echo's, Jane's, and Cosmos's eyes all became unfocused then suddenly super sharp, distinct, and quick.

There was a minor downside to astral-projecting, with the added perception you were more likely to fall for feints. Moyra knew Jane and Cosmos tried to minimize the handicap by drawing in their wraiths to only their weapons' maximum reach. In the many times she had been trained dueling by Jane over the years, she had only won twice, once when her father distracted Jane by sending a small boomerang around them, the second time when their duel had disturbed a pheasant nesting in the grass where they had dueled.

But the upsides to astral projection far outweighed anything so trivial. Extrasensory perception, speed, strength, and supernatural reflexes often said to be precognition.

Jane went through the door first, dart straw at the ready and exotic sword partly drawn. Cosmos followed four paces behind her; after going through the door, he waited at one side for Echo. They continued side by side. Moyra brought up the rear several paces back, arrow nocked but not drawn so that her arm wouldn't tier.

After Cosmos and Echo moved farther in the room, Moyra realized they were going down; the roof was distancing from their heads. She identified training dummies in the center of the room. The first set were in a triangle formation, complete with spears, shields, and armor. The next, set at the halfway point of the room, were four plain wooden dummies, each with a single wooden leg, a swivel waist, and a barrel chest with two arms. They were set up a few paces apart and encircled an empty space. Jane was crouched beside the last at the far side of the room; it was the simplest of all the dummies, just a wide post with pegs half an arm's reach long up and down its length. *This was supposed to be a storage building. They must have abducted its occupants and made it their forward headquarters*, Moyra thought.

Signaling for everyone to hold their positions, Jane went up some steps at the far side of the room and stepped through another door. Cosmos and Echo hid at the trio of dummies; Moyra went back through the doorway and closed it, all but a crack. *If this is where I'm going to be fighting from, I want to make sure nobody comes up behind me.* Taking the rusty helmet from the third closet, she rushed to the far door and gingerly hung it so that if anyone so much as cracked open the door behind her, it would fall. As she made her way back across the room, she noticed one of the crates had glass panes labeled on it. She pried the crate open, removed a pane, and placed it under the helmet. Hoping her trap didn't take too long, she rushed back to her post and peeked out the cracked door.

After a few short moments, the far door crashed down and out, Jane riding it down the steps feet first, taking a few running steps then veering off to one side and doubling back to the wall. Putting a dart in the cylinder weapon, she raised it to her mouth and waited.

Moyra could see what looked like a large animal rushing on all fours toward the now permanently open doorway. There were at least four people chasing after it; she had hoped they would only face four people total. It leaped out the doorway, spreading its wings, looking for the life of her just like a flying fox. As it glided over the lowered room, it looked behind each training dummy. Its glide was getting lower just before it got to the last set of dummies, Moyra drew her bow and kneed open the door, shooting it in the center of the back.

"*Ouch!*" it screamed with a very human expression of pain.

Moyra willed herself to think of it as an animal. She had more than half-expected to hear an animalistic roar after seeing the way it moved on all fours, combined with the fact that the disguise was very convincing. The abductor cringed up its whole body in pain, crashing head first. As it crashed, the mask/helmet turned all the way around, bone breaking. Moyra turned her head away before the head of the disguise rolled free. Watching Cosmos and Echo run safely to Jane's aid, Moyra knew she took the only course of action she could live with.

Jane was fighting two spear wielders and a swordsman. A second bare-chested swordsman was collapsed halfway down the steps. To Moyra's surprise, the garb each of the spear wielders had on was that of those guarding the city. She was curious to know if they were turncoat guards collaborating with the abductors or the same enemies simply donning yet another disguise.

Cosmos throw daggers, doing little more than distract them as he and Echo charged to Jane's aid. Her assailants doubled their effort to kill her before the new foes could engage. The distraction was successful; one spear wielder who got a dagger in the arm charged at Jane carelessly. She stabbed him through the leg, and an instant before the swordsman could decapitate her, she lopped off his weapon hand. The second spear wielder stabbed her in the hip, but she jumped back just then, and it looked like her armor served its purpose.

Moyra rushed into the room but stopped and drew her bow when she saw two more men with spears. The first was bald, and the second had a heavy head of hair mostly covered by a helm. She fired an arrow. The first of the two threw his spear toward Cosmos and Echo, and then Moyra's arrow struck the door frame to his side. His spear was deftly deflected by Cosmos yet still struck in front of Echo, who nimbly leaped over it. Moyra shot a second arrow; it struck the helmed man in the chest plate, causing a loud, resounding ring. The arrow made a dent and possibly a small hole but ricocheted, not penetrating to his flesh.

Jane disengaged as Cosmos arrived in a flurry of flashing blades and Echo placed himself in between Jane and the two wounded fighters. The one-handed swordsman prudently recoiled, clutching his bloody stump, but didn't retreat far. Although the wounded spear wielder knelt and clutched his leg weakly with his wounded arm, he foolishly threw his spear at Jane.

Echo knocked it down hard with his sword and stabbed with his dagger in one-fluid motion, slaying him.

Moyra was distressed at how dispassionately Echo took a life for the first time but couldn't let any subjective feelings hold sway because she was fully aware that they were fighting for their lives. *It's harder to kill with an arrow because you don't feel the immediate threat of death or the natural self-preservation instinct to strike first*, thought Moyra. *But on the other side of the same coin, it can be easier in that you don't fight face-to-face or feel your blade penetrate their flesh.*

The bald new foe swept up the sword from the man collapsed on the steps and, without missing a step, joined the melee, attacking Cosmos alongside the unharmed spear wielder Jane had previously been fighting. Moyra rushed a few steps with her arrow drawn then shot at the helmeted spear wielder yet again, this time closer, with her arrow flying a more direct path and her bow drawn as hard as she could she hoped to sunder his armor. Her last attack got his full attention though, and he raised his shield as soon as she started to draw. The shield was angled perfectly, and the arrow was rendered perfectly harmless.

Jane used the cylinder to send a dart at the rump of the man whose hand she'd severed as he was trying to retrieve his sword by stepping on the thumb and prying the fingers free. He had a look of supreme surprise before stumbling two steps and collapsing.

Echo shivered noticeably as he pulled his dagger from the eye of the man he'd slain. Moyra was glad that he wasn't as unemotional to this as she had previously feared. *Unfortunately it only gets easier each time. I wish killing was not something that people became callused to*, she thought sadly.

The spear wielder left Cosmos to his bald companion and sought to exact vengeance on Echo. Cosmos rolled his sword under the bald man's sword, stabbing under his arm. Baldy slashed his shield at Cosmos's face Cosmos leaned back, hooking his dagger on the shield, pulled himself forward, and swept the bald man's feet out from under him with his foot. He dropped his sword and grasped Cosmos's leg with both arms; he effectively pinned him there. Moyra was sure it was a desperate death hold as blood poured from under his arm down Cosmos's leg.

Jane reengaged in the melee, attacking the helmed foe who had been Moyra's target. She dodged a spear thrust to her face; as she moved down its length, she grabbed its shaft with her empty left hand. Annoyed, he bashed at her knee with his shield; she kicked it wide and thrust with her sword. He smirked contemptuously at her badly chosen target for his heart was covered by chest-plate armor. His insolent smile vanished when her exotic blue sword struck the exact place Moyra's arrow had hit earlier. The thrust went all the way through him with a heavy dull *thud* against the inside back of his armor.

Jane pulled her blade free from his armor and unsheathed her dagger, throwing it at the last foe as he chased a frantic Echo. Echo had apparently been far outmatched, having lost his wraith after killing for the first time. His pursuer put on a burst of speed, outdistancing Jane's dagger and two from Cosmos. Moyra noted Echo's course; he was running for the encirclement of training dummies. She released an arrow at Echo's pursuer; it grazed the high neck of his armor. He slowed, flashed a look of anger that promised she was next, then continued his pursuit.

"Evade!" Jane shouted. Echo scrunched his shoulders, bobbed, and weaved. A spear flashed by him, sundering the nearest training dummy. Echo ran past the defeated dummy through the clearing and out the other side of the encirclement. The spear wielder retrieved his weapon, shaking with rage, as Echo went around the dummies, returning to the twins.

Jane smiled broadly, giving Echo congratulatory claps on the shoulder and telling him he did well. "I was afraid you were going to die on me like the others, but you heeded my training well," Jane said, embracing Echo.

Moyra was surprised by the action and more so to see Jane's eyes glistening, threatening to send tears down her cheeks. Surely, Echo was her only trainee; she couldn't remember Jane ever having apprentices other than in the limited capacity that Jane instructed Moyra in their duels. Jane must have meant those who romantically pursued her when she mentioned others. Moyra knew that a childhood friend whom Jane liked died long ago and that Husain, her father's guard who died two years ago, had shown interest in Jane. But unless there was something more recent, she found it unlikely that her friend, always cool and collected, would become emotional. Remembering Bella's tale of abductors having attacked a group Jane had been in and Jane's reluctance to refuse the use of poison, Moyra understood Jane's sensitive state.

The spear wielder started moving toward Moyra; she instinctively stepped back and pulled an arrow from her quiver. Then forcing her legs to move diagonally forward to her friends, Moyra kept watch on him; it occurred to her that he was making for the door not her.

"Moyra, we cannot let him escape. If the ambush outside has not already succeeded, he could ruin everything," said Cosmos.

Moyra released her arrow, but the spear wielder got his plate gauntlets up first. Guarding his face and neck, he also stepped left. She expected his change of direction from watching his feet carefully, but his raised guard caused the arrow to only cut the side of his face and ear. She retreated toward the door, preparing to shoot again as he and Cosmos rushed toward her. They all knew she wouldn't get another shot. Cosmos threw daggers at and before the spear wielder. He ducked the first and ignored the latter, not allowing distractions.

Find a way, Moyra. Don't let this be the end, she thought desperately. Crouching, she blocked a downward blow of the spear with the bow. Once she felt the full weight of the attack, she leaped forward with an upward thrust of the arrow in her opposite hand. It connected with the center of his neck, striking hard against bone then penetrating the far side. The surprise in his eyes matched hers. How could this foe who survived unscathed against Jane and Cosmos fall to her? Sure, they were fighting multiple opponents at the time, and he must have expected her to follow Echo's example to flee, not to stand her ground, but it felt surreal, regardless of having been underestimated. Paralyzed, the spear wielder dropped his weapon and fell on his back.

Cosmos took Moyra by the hand, leading her past the dummies up the steps and into the far room, not wanting her to hear her paralyzed victim's last breaths gargled and drowning. This room was much like the first room they had entered, too much junk and too little space for it. There were many crates lining each side of a path making a hall to the door on the opposite of the room. The crates held the junk back, allowing a better walkway than the first room had. No longer having to hold the illusion of a storage building, these bags and crates had been plundered of their most valuable items. Many empty bags and opened crates could be seen among the jumble of stuffs. The shelves weren't collapsed from overcapacity like the first room, either, but were mostly empty except for the bedding on them.

Moyra found comfort in Cosmos's hand; her breathing became even, and she no longer felt like she was going to be relived of the contents of her stomach.

"You seem to have relaxed," Cosmos said, giving her a wan smile. "This next room should be the last. I wonder what we will find." He opened the door to the room at that end of the building.

The immediate area of the last room was for dining; it had a heavy wooden table with a bench on either side on the far side of the room. There was an area separated by a half wall that had a bar and stools on one side; the other side had a small kitchen with a stove oven and a sink. As they looked over the room, they saw a large man with gray hair lying on his back near the table, dead. He had a gaping wound in his chest, a wooden spoon handle in between his teeth, and foam coming out his mouth.

"She promised," Moyra said bitterly, remembering Jane's promises to only use the sleep poison.

"It was an accident," Jane explained as she silently came into the room. "My first dart was intercepted. It hit the mask of the strange one in disguise. I loaded another without looking because I had to dodge his darts. I escaped so suddenly I did not know what kind of dart I hit him with until the next time I loaded." Jane talked with her back turned as she experimentally lifted the wing of a disguise hanging on the wall. "But in all honesty, I do not regret it. I probably would if I had to watch the whole thing all over again no matter whom it was used on. Even a rabid animal deserves a better death than they have given many."

Hearing the pain in Jane's voice, Moyra couldn't help but feel sorry for her. The emotional torment her dear friend had been through was indeed worthy of the name *Sorrow*.

As Jane's shoulders shook in silent sobs, Cosmos loosened his hand on Moyra's, but she released first. Going to comfort her friend, Moyra knew this was just the most recent in a long line of trauma Jane had endured. Considering that they didn't even hesitate to mercy-kill their own associate when in the throes of their terrible poison, Moyra was sure the memory of a friend or loved one dying in that way, with no means of helping them, would be grave indeed.

"Did that sound like glass breaking to you just now?" Cosmos asked, looking at Jane.

Jane nodded.

Moyra didn't hear it, but she snapped to attention, remembering the trap she had set up. "Somebody has come in the building! I set a pane of glass to break if the door was opened."

Cosmos was out the door and across the hall of the next room by the time Jane and Moyra had untangled themselves and followed.

"That was good thinking. I am glad you are with us. Even if our allies are the most likely to follow, it is good to have a warning," Jane praised Moyra as they ran past Echo who was tying up the foes Jane got with sleeping darts. "Cosmos and I think so much alike we seldom say something that is not already on the tip of the other's tongue. It is good to have somebody around that bounces fresh ideas past us."

Cosmos pulled opened the door that had closed under its own weight at the far side of the indoor training grounds. Then he leaned way back and turned his head aside, dodging an attack that was intended to cave in his skull. Moyra stopped in her tracks, holding her breath in fright as a war hammer swiped through the air where Cosmos's head had been an instant before.

"Whoa! Ha-ha!" Cosmos exclaimed, taking a few steps back and regaining his balance.

The man at the door looked over the room dumbstruck, holding his weapon in two burly hands. He looked like a younger brother to the dead man in the back room. He was as big and had nearly identical facial features, though his hair had much less gray in it than the other man's did.

"Surprise! And welcome home." Cosmos said the first word dramatically, raising his arms high and wide.

Then the latter was dangerously drawing his weapons and taunting him, daring him to come in. "Rajiv! Rajiv! Are you hurt? Have you been captured?" he exclaimed desperately, taking a step forward. He paused as though seeing his ready opposition for the first time. "Or have you been killed?" he asked directing the question toward Cosmos.

"We will let you have him back if you tell us where the *Clytemnestra* has set off to," Jane said unthreateningly, coming to a stop beside Cosmos with her weapons in their sheaths.

"Dead then," he concluded, taking Jane's offer as a declaration of the fact. Setting his jaw, he looked to their faces for denial or conformation but got none.

Moyra, sensing action, aimed her arrow. He surprised her by grabbing the door with one hand and pulling it. Cosmos rushed him, and he thrust his hammer with one hand. Cosmos dodged to the side, hooking his curved dagger on the hammerhead, and pulled. Moyra shot at his head; he leaned back, overpowering Cosmos, and pulled his weapon free. An instant later, the arrow struck the door, helping it close.

"Do we pursue or fortify here?" Cosmos asked, deferring to Jane. There was a crash in the next room, which helped Jane decide.

"Pursue! He is trying to delay us. There may still be fighting going on outside." Jane opened the door then kicked it closed again before Cosmos could go through, but not before Moyra could glimpse a man on the far side of the room holding a hammer and wearing a fox head helmet. She instinctively released her arrow and was annoyed when it hit the door above her last arrow. Two lesser *thuds* could be heard against the opposite side of the door as the darts shot from his helmet hit the closed door.

Echo retrieved the shields from the nearby trio of training dummies. "How about the three of us use these to rush him and Moyra cover fire from behind?" Echo asked, presenting the shields helpfully.

Cosmos cast a worried glance at Moyra but said nothing.

"Good idea, but you should stay behind to shield Moyra. Besides, you are too tall, and the roof is low in there, so it would be harder for her to shoot over you." Jane said, revaluating the situation after seeing the worry on Cosmos's face. Cosmos gave Jane a grateful nod and took a shield offered by Echo.

Cosmos took point when Jane opened the door. After two running steps, he had to jump over the three sacks that had been torn from the closet. Moyra released an arrow when he landed before Jane could follow. It struck the far door just as it was slammed closed.

"Blast! I'm sick of my arrows hitting doors," said Moyra, annoyed.

Jane smiled at her and then rushed after Cosmos. Echo and Moyra followed at a slower pace, ready for action if the door opened again.

"Hurry, he is escaping!" Cosmos yelled, slamming open the door after looking through.

When Moyra got to the door, she saw an abandoned fox helmet on the ground and a chariot fleeing with their adversary at the reins. A disguised abductor lay on the floor at his feet.

"Help us!" called a spear wielder off to the side. He lay on his back in the lamp light. His arm and leg were broken badly, probably from the war-hammer foe who had just escaped. Two dead abductors could be seen at the edge of the light. Another guard sat leaned up against the other lamppost, sweating and rubbing at his eyes. Among the many injured and unmoving bodies, he was the one whom Jane rushed to aid.

"Leave him. He just has blinding powder in his eyes. Help me with this man," Moyra said after noticing the yellow powder on his face.

"No, he has been poisoned. It is not very bad. He must have pulled the dart before it could spread much poison," Jane said, forcing him to lie down. "Echo, run to the river and soak a cloth. Bring it back seeping wet. Don't wring it out."

"Just grazed my neck, but it burns, and I closed my eyes when the powder was thrown, yet my vision became blurry anyway." Moyra heard the injured man saying as she prepared to try and set the arm of the man she was helping.

"Cosmos, help me set his arm." Moyra looked around. "Cosmos?"

"He is in pursuit, of course," Jane replied when Moyra looked at her in askance. Taking a wet cloth from Echo, she washed his neck and wiped his face, then Jane tugged his shirt collar up so it would hold the cold, wet cloth in place on his neck. The poisoned man started breathing fast and shaking. "No no no! Not the convulsions. Breath steady, relax. Echo, help me get his armor off," Jane commanded.

Echo just stood there frozen with fright.

"Help him please!" the man at Moyra's side said, pushing her toward Jane with his good hand.

As she unbuckled the straps on the side and shoulder of his armor, she remembered standing with Cosmos as they released their wraiths then how his pain subsided as their auras mingled. She decided to try that though she knew it was unlikely his wraith would be susceptive to hers. She knew everyone had a wraith, despite Jane's denial of the fact, but few people's wraiths were receptive to each other. Trying to relax, she concentrated and called her wraith. Most people had exceedingly weak auras, and the few people with exceedingly strong auras like Jane and Cosmos would never feel them.

"What are you planning?" Jane asked suspiciously. Because she was still astral-projecting, she could feel Moyra's wraith push up against hers.

"Earlier, when Cosmos's and my aura's mingled, his pain subsided. I know I'm just grasping at the wind here, but I thought I would try it again," Moyra replied. "Echo, please go soak another cloth then get a bucket for water if you can find one."

Jane stared at Moyra in awe. "But surely this man doesn't have an astral projection. Mine is the strongest. I have ever heard of excluding berserkers, and I cannot feel his."

"Most people are extremely weak, and the stronger yours is, the less likely you are to feel them. Unless you are extremely charismatic, people with a lot of charisma tend to be more sensitive and receptive to others." As Moyra explained, she tried to feel his aura but got no impressions. So she decided to try and force her wraith in him like she had read of berserkers doing long ago; they called the healing technique as sharing pain. She immediately felt his suffering, pain, and burning itchiness; the irritating sensation made her want to scratch her whole body.

"You are sweating," Jane said, but Moyra hardly heard her. After a while, he stopped convulsing, and she thought his pain may have lessened slightly.

Distantly, she noticed Captain Sanders arrive and people moving around them as she shared the poisoned man's pain. Wondering if he would die or pull through, Moyra thought it would be more likely she'd lose consciousness first.

Finally, Moyra couldn't take it anymore. She drew in her wraith, got up without a word, and walked to Jane's horse. She thought that Jane might have helped her up onto the saddle, but as she rode back to the inn, everything except bed and sleep seemed trivial.

REVELATIONS
AT THE BRIDGE

Following the chariot as quietly as he could, Cosmos thought he had lost it several times. The dreary fog and moonless night made it impossible to follow by sight; indeed, most of the time it was hard to see past his outstretched arm in the gloomy darkness. He listened intently while keeping eyes turned to the ground directly in front of his horse. Often, all he would have to follow was the distant sound of the chariot going over uneven ground or brush and the rattle of short lightweight spears meant to be thrown from the chariot.

As they traveled to higher ground, the fog lessened, but Cosmos kept his distance. This was about more than defeat and capture; they had defeated many and captured some. He needed to know where the attacks were coming from and more importantly where they were taking the captives. He distantly heard the chariot pull onto the highway, and as he neared, he was surprised not to hear it pull off the other side. The chariot followed the highway southwest toward the bridge that went over the Aroostook River. Cosmos had been sure they would go to the cliffs that run north and south along the eastern edge of Brunswick. He followed silently, riding in the soft earth beside the road.

"Whoa!" the chariot driver called, coming to a stop before crossing the bridge.

Cosmos came to a stop too, dismounted, and ran closer to the chariot on silent feet. Just as he got close enough to make out their shapes on the back of the chariot, the driver pulled the mask off his companion.

"Come on, wake up, Kei. I'm sure the spear shaft just hit you at the back of the head," he said slapping the younger man on the cheek.

"Ouch! Stop, I'm awake. What happened? How did they find us?" Kei asked, painfully cracking his neck to one side. "Ouch," he said again, holding his hand at the back of his head and neck. "I'll poison five of them for each and every one of us they killed, condemning those to excruciating deaths beyond their imaginations!" Kei said maliciously with all the venom of a viper.

Cosmos wanted to attack them in surprise then and there but waited patiently, absorbing every word while lying beside the road.

"They got Rajiv," was the older man's only reply. He dropped the head of the disguise; it rolled off the end of the chariot and landed on the highway.

"Are you sure?" Kei asked, hooking a three long-fingered claw-tipped wing on the side of the chariot and standing up. "Robert would have warned us if they were bringing enough guards down to do that. Counting Rajiv, there were eight men in there, and the four of us outside makes twelve."

Kei shook his head in denial, wrapped his wings around himself, and turned to face his companion.

"Rajiv is as good as you are. They would have had to outnumber them two to one and have a hell of a surprise attack. Not to mention you killed that suspicious lieutenant last night in the guard tower. Robert said he was the best of them," the older man explained.

So their attack on the guard tower was not to capture people but to silence a single suspicious lieutenant. Cosmos remembered hearing them from his vantage point at the docks saying much the same. At least one of the Spearwielder Guard thought outside the narrow box their captain put them in, but he was killed for his trouble.

"Robert's the only reason either of us are alive. He killed his fellow guard that attacked you. Otherwise, you would have been a head shorter and not have just been knocked out. Then he threw blinding powder at those attacking me. Even then, I was overwhelmed, but one of them attacked Robert. I was the last one standing—Robert is dead."

Kei was quiet for a while apparently, letting the revelation sink in.

Cosmos felt a small measure of sympathy for Captain Sanders. Traitors like Robert could have made his job near impossible. He remembered that many of the abductors they just confronted had city guard's uniforms weapons and armor on. He had thought they were just wearing the disguises they would use to get into the city with. But what if they had all been traitors, lying to and manipulating those whom they fought beside, only to stab them in the back at a critical moment?

"What of those inside?" Kei asked soberly. Cosmos edged along the side of the road and still had to strain his ears to hear the hushed reply.

"Dead—all dead. Rajiv is the only one I didn't see. Them mercenaries, what done, it just took four, and not one of them looked injured." the older man replied, sounding shaken.

He must not have noticed the rope on the two Echo tied up, or he would have known they were not all dead, thought Cosmos.

"Is there anyone from the mercenaries' guild we could impersonate? Do you know if maybe someone has been away for a long time, collecting bounties in another realm? Any means we can think of to mislead them and set their plans amuck will be like twisting a dagger in their back!" Kei said excitedly as though he was uplifting his companion's moral. "Come on, Kahn! Think of Auriok, Robert, Rajiv, and all the others. Think of a way, and together I'll help you end them!" The pleasure in his voice at the thought of vengeance was malevolent.

"I don't like that idea but, sometime ago, I heard their champion was in the south, working as a body-guard for the feudal lord who controls the salt mines of Lorneoin," Kahn said, sounding unconvinced.

Cosmos knew of what he spoke—the feudal lord was Moyra's father, and the champion was, of course,

Jane. Moyra's father, Avigdor Sublime, had come to the guild over three years before and asked for the most competent female fighter to be his daughter's "minder." Abdulla, the weapon master, was amusing himself by making Cosmos fight six men with a variety of weapons at that time. Cosmos was doing okay; they fought with reed bundled practice swords, staves, and a pair of nasty wooden morning star.

He had gotten them down to four, then Moyra's old man, who recognized that Cosmos was astral-projecting, got a bright idea. He threw one of the few small boomerangs that he kept on his person at Cosmos from behind. Cosmos, distracted, attacked the boomerang that would have flown harmlessly around his head, and he received many red welts and swollen joints from his attackers for his trouble. He almost laughed at the painful memory before remembering where he was. Cosmos regretted that he never left Moyra's father with a better first impression. Cosmos had been fumingly angry; although Abdulla and the acting guild master, Cosmos's and Jane's eldest brother, Derek, laughed it off as a good joke.

"That could work. Those salt mines are so far south they may as well be in another realm," Kei replied, but before his idea could gain momentum, Kahn headed him off.

"No, it wouldn't work. Most everyone in that guild is family. It's one thing to impersonate a guard or visiting dignitary. But do you think you could pass yourself off as an uncle, cousin, brother, or father?" Kahn asked skeptically. Cosmos mentally added *Or sister* mockingly, realizing how little they knew of the person they would impersonate. "No, we should go with my first instinct before the ship gets too far down river," Kahn said, turning his attention to the horses. "Besides, those Salaamed sailors aren't likely to sit idle once they learn their comrades have been taken from their ship."

"Aw, I don't mind gliding downriver and landing on a moving boat so much. But I'll have to climb those dastardly chains to the top of the bridge pillars if I'm going to get enough distance to catch it," Kei complained, referring to the long sloped chains almost wide enough to walk up that supported the spans in between support pliers. He stooped low and picked up his fox-head helmet from the road while still on the chariot with three long-fingered claws. They looked awkward, always bent like hooks.

"Getty up!" Kahn said, slapping the reins against the chariot horses.

Cosmos searched around for his horse but could not find him and thought Eclipse must have wandered down to the river. So without looking too hard, he followed on foot, fearing he had lost his chance to confront them. It was bad in and of itself that the boat escaped with the captives. Cosmos could not add to that failure by letting Kei tell them of tonight's exploits. Luckily, they had not stopped far from the bridge; if he ran fast and they spoke for a moment before Kei climbed the chain, he might yet have a chance to confront them. *I must not let them have their way*, Cosmos thought repeatedly as he pursued them.

The sun started to rise just as he got to the bridge, its yellow raze shining on the tops of the tall pillars of the bridge. The bridge was above the thickest part of the fog; everything was still hazy though. He stopped and bent over, resting his hands on his knees to catch his breath before running again. He had not seen the chariot returning yet, so hopefully Kei had not started climbing the angled support chain. Minutes later, he saw the chariot stopped up ahead with only one person on it. He instinctively looked for the other around the chariot, at the edge of the bridge, and, as he got closer, up the load-bearing chain. Cosmos did not find Kei right away, but following Kahn's gaze, he spotted him. About three times Kahn's height, up the chain hung a dark shape. Those long claws he had thought looked awkward seemed appropriate for their current task.

The chariot started pulling away in a wide turn to double back. Cosmos put on a burst of speed, focusing on the climbing figure. As he approached the chain, he did not stop or even slow. Drawing his kukris dagger with his right hand and grasping the tail of his cloak with his left, he ran up the wide taunt chain. His weight was insignificant compared to the weight the chain was already supporting; he doubted it would even vibrate as he ran up. He did not know if he was wrong about it vibrating or if Kei had just heard his footsteps coming up. But the fox-head helmet capable of shooting those horrifying poison darts of anguish turned toward him.

Cosmos pulled his cloak taunt in front of him with his left hand, protecting his head and upper body. He could feel two impacts against his cloak as he ran blindly forward and up. Not trusting a third shot to be as poorly placed or himself to keep placing his feet accurately, he threw his kukris dagger with his right hand and rolled forward on his right shoulder off the opposite side of the chain. Cosmos heard his dagger impact with his unseen target but could not look because his immediate landing required all his attention. He grasped a chain link with his right hand, helping to direct his landing, but let go at once because pain told him the awkward angle threatened to pull his shoulder out of socket.

The expression on Kahn's face as Cosmos landed in a crouch from his long fall with blood showering in between them was of horror and dreadful hatred.

"I will not let you do as you please!" Cosmos proclaimed, pulling his sword with his right hand. His confidence faltered, realizing how close he had come to dislocating his shoulder. It had actually dislocated for an instant before he let go of the chain but snapped back into socket at an awkward angle. His grasp on his sword was barely strong enough to keep it from clanging to his feet. He did not even dare rotate his arm so he could grasp the sword with two hands for fear he would lose it in that instant.

"Who…who are you?" Kahn asked.

Cosmos felt his sword slipping, so he flexed his fist. The pain brought unushered tears to his eyes. "I am Sorrow," Cosmos replied simply. As if on cue, the tears ran down his cheeks. He was starting to feel the clown, legs shaking, sword about to fall to the ground, and to top it all off, he was crying. He decided to bluff. "The Bane of Kahn," he finished lamely.

"I'm…" Kahn started to say something, possibly to introduce himself, but seemed to think better of it upon realizing Cosmos was referring to him. There was a flash of a different emotion on his face, maybe remorse or sympathy. The compunction was gone, returning to the stone face of hatred, so soon that Cosmos doubted he had even seen it. The blood sprays pressure gradually lessened to a steady pour. Cosmos's stomach turned as he heard whimpering up above.

"What is your plan for the captives? I cannot imagine you have a use for that many people even as slaves. What realm are you selling them too?" Cosmos asked, knowing Jane would demand answers were she in his place.

Kahn raised his reins as if to slap the horses into motion. Cosmos's shoulder was tingling and fingers going numb; he heard his sword tip touch stone. Cosmos reached across with his left hand and awkwardly switched sword hands. It was like touching a stranger's hand; his right hand hardly registered contact.

Kahn hesitated, watching Cosmos wiggle his fingers and rotate his shoulder painfully.

"How about the disguises? Why bats? Do they represent something beyond the possibility of the captives being eaten?" Cosmos asked, trying a different approach, worried Kahn would escape on the chariot.

"You treat your servants like slaves, what's it matter that we appropriate them and use them like you do in all but name?" Kahn said, choosing to reply to the first question.

It was true that most of the people they took were servants, which were missed less than people who actively work among the community. The highest rooms of a building were almost always the least comfortable, and servants who lived with their employer often stayed there. But Cosmos was sure they took travelers and even merchant convoys when they could manage it.

"Servants may not be paid enough to easily rise above their station. But they have family, intimate domestic lives. Conformity is their choice, and they have the freedom to change their lives as they see fit," Cosmos replied easily because his mother had been a servant for many years before choosing to start a family with his father. His arm was not getting much better; something felt pinched in the joint of his shoulder.

"Youngster, you're not as tough as you think," Kahn said. He sounded pleased that Cosmos was injured, regardless of it being minor.

"That is for sure," Cosmos replied. Kahn seemed surprised by how readily Cosmos agreed. *I feel invincible most of the time. It is only after being injured that I learn the truth of my mortality*, thought Cosmos feeling vulnerable.

Kei stopped whimpering. Cosmos dared a look up. The kukris dagger he received from Avigdor was, of course, perfectly balanced but also weighty and its edge intense enough to breach the most obdurate chain mail at the seams. Yet he was still surprised to see Kei's left arm cleaved from his side, even though he wore no armor. Hanging awkwardly by clawed limbs, it had not taken long for him to bleed to death with a gaping hole so close to his heart. Cosmos heard the rattle of the spears in their bucket compartment on the chariot and looked to Kahn just in time to dodge a thrown spear.

"I may not get a better chance to murder one of you mercenaries injured and alone as you are," Kahn said, considering Cosmos then looking ahead, torn between fight and flight or possibly making sure he was alone.

Cosmos threw a dagger with his weakened right arm and strafed quickly in the opposite direction Kahn was looking. The dagger flew short, hitting the side of the chariot and fell harmlessly to the bridge. Cosmos doubled his speed trying to stay ahead of Kahn gaze. Pulling another dagger from a left leg sheath as it crossed his path, continuing to rotate, spinning to overcome the inertia of his shoulder, and snapping his arm out, he let fly the dagger. It clipped Kahn on the side of his head behind the ear as he tried to dodge. "Blast you, Sorrow! I can't take my eyes off you for a second," Kahn cursed angrily, taking up his war hammer and abandoning the chariot.

"You should have known that much without a demonstration," Cosmos chided, keeping the distance between them and circling so the rising sun was at his back.

Kahn stopped following, taking a wide stance, and squaring off. Then taking short fast breaths, his eyes lost focus only for an instant; next, he came at Cosmos with renewed vigor. Two long, fast strides closed the distance. Cosmos took a half step to one side and turned, barely avoiding an underhand swing that would have taken out his knee, and did not stop until meeting his face. Then stabbing with a dagger, which his right hand had unconsciously found, his aim was fast and his strike true, hitting the chain-mail seam under Kahn's left arm, but his grip was pathetic. Cosmos's hand slid down the dagger grip and along the blade. He flinched back with a bloody hand at the same time, taking an elbow to the face from Kahn. Cosmos staggered away, barely avoiding a cross-down swing of the war hammer that broke a flagstone when it hit the bridge.

Kahn did not continue attacking; he just sighed raised his left arm and slapped free the loosely hanging dagger from under his arm. "If only you had the full strength of your right arm, that would have been a critical hit," Kahn commented. He seemed unperturbed by the near-death hit; on the contrary, he was composed and contented because Cosmos was the one injured in the attempt. That worried Cosmos because even if he could hit Kahn ten times to his one, which seemed very unlikely at this point, one glancing blow of the war hammer to his knee or just about anywhere really would bring an end to this farce.

"I suppose my handicap makes us just about even," Cosmos said with as much bravado as he could muster, but the statement sounded erroneous even to his own ears.

"Pahaha, that's the spirit! Keep telling yourself that. You've got more bluster than common sense. It's twice as hard to attack as to defend. Let's see you put that boasting into action. Come at me, Sorrow!" Kahn taunted, holding his hammer angled low to the ground in his right hand, taking a left step forward, and he signaled "Come" with his other large burly hand tauntingly. Kahn was an intimidating figure in his shining half-plate armor over chainmail.

"Remember you asked for it," said Cosmos, already on the offensive.

As Cosmos moved forward, he pulled daggers from two of the twenty-four dagger sheaths covering his armor. He threw one just as Kahn started to swing his hammer; Kahn sidestepped, avoiding it. The action caused his hammer to swing faster; Cosmos delayed imperceptibly, allowing the hammer pass within a breath of him. Aiming for Kahn's right elbow, he chopped down, trying to sever the limb; Kahn jerked his arm back, blocking with his gauntlet and handle. Cosmos reversed his blade, stepping closer. He sliced toward Kahn's neck and face. Kahn spun away, pushing Cosmos back with his hammer.

"Humph! Rajiv wouldn't fall to such simple attacks. Come at me like you did him. Show me what you can do," Kahn said in annoyance.

"Sorry, I have not taken you seriously, or maybe it is this injury I am underestimating." Cosmos had already astral-projected long enough that night to have an impressive store of vigor. So he had not intended to astral project while facing this single opponent wielding a slow, heavy war hammer. Not to mention the side effect some people experienced when astral-projecting in battle for too long—trance. The dazed state was often a warning sign of what was to come short-term memory loss and unpleasant flashbacks.

"You know that the time for bluffing is over—now you'll die," Kahn said, advancing menacingly. But he stopped abruptly, feeling Cosmos's wraith the moment Cosmos started astral-projecting.

Cosmos only knew that was why he stopped because he could feel his opponent's wraith as well. Cosmos remembered Kahn's eyes becoming unfocused just before attacking and realized in hindsight that was when he started astral-projecting. Few people could astral-project, except by chance when they seldom happened to dream-walk, and fewer still were trained to make uses of it in combat. Along with the normal jubilation of heightened senses that came when astral-projecting, the pain in Cosmos's shoulder increased as well. The pain was greater than when he first momentarily dislocated it dropping from the chain, but at least this time, tears did not accompany the pain, though he nearly dropped his dagger.

"There are disadvantages in every benefit if one knows where to look," said Kahn. He attacked in a rush, having obviously noticed the dagger nearly slip from Cosmos's fingers.

They clashed. Cosmos's sword rang repeatedly off Kahn's armor but never found flesh, and Kahn's hammer swept dangerously close but never got so much as a glancing blow. Cosmos put his dagger into an empty sheath above his waist on his back but never let go of the handle, taking up a one-handed sword stance. Standing side face with his left hand forward, Cosmos would thrust and retreat; parrying the heavy-hammer swings was impossible. But he put his sword up to block many times, with no intention of stopping or redirecting the war hammer; he just used the contact to help speed himself out of its way. Kahn's well-made, heavy half-plate armor had not a dent even after repeatedly thrusting his sword against it, only shallow scratches almost imperceptible. Cosmos doubted a heavy spear with a fine point could sunder it much less his sword.

Cosmos had no more luck penetrating Kahn's chain mail than his shining half-plate armor. The sword was too thick and wide to succeed where his thin sharp dagger had failed. Kahn attacked ruthlessly, giving little thought to defense, relying on his armor to serve its purpose. Cosmos retreated more often than not, feeling that his attack power was cut in half because he could only fight with one hand. He relied on foot techniques to outmaneuver Kahn. Sometimes he would just change their course enough to put the sun in his eyes; other times, he would deviously take half steps and turns so he could attack from behind. *Kahn has obviously never known such a wily opponent*, Cosmos thought as one such subterfuge allowed him to strike Kahn with a thrust behind the ear in the same place his dagger hit before Kahn had abandoned the chariot.

The smile on Kahn's face showed it was not a good hit and alerted Cosmos to his folly. Kahn had done some maneuvering of his own, cutting off Cosmos's obvious escape with the bridge's support chain.

Kahn's counterattack was fast and sure; all Cosmos had time for was to block. The heavy war hammer and powerful two-handed attack was too much to be blocked Cosmos was forced back hard. His back hit the chain as solid as a wall. The hammer came on the sword notwithstanding. Unable to resist, his sword started to cut into his armor. Cosmos rotated his wrist, turning the blade sideways so that it would not cut into his flesh. His sword slapped against him diagonally across his chest from his half raised left hand to his right shoulder. All that took place in an instant a lesser opponent would have been cut in half by his own blade.

With his right hand clutching the dagger in the sheath on his lower back, his shoulder jarred painfully from impact front and back. To Cosmos's great surprise and relief, the pain of his shoulder lessened immediately after that. Kahn kept pressure on his hammer against Cosmos's chest pinning his sword in place. He thrust his face in front of Cosmos, grinning malevolently. Cosmos desperately pulled his dagger and stabbed Kahn in the side of the head.

His wicked grin never left his face even in death or when he fell down against the stone bridge.

Later, after retrieving his weapons and the two dead bodies, Cosmos drove the chariot along the bridge. The risen sun dispersed the fog into nothingness, even along the river and both of its banks. Cosmos was surprised to see Jane riding his horse, Eclipse. She was surprised to see him too, sighing noticeably in relief. A drowsy Echo followed her, guiding an unsaddled Cayenne by the reins. Cosmos left the bridge and steered the chariot off the side of the steep highway bank, coming to a stop beside them. They had obviously been following his footprints in the soft earth beside the highway.

"I feared the worst when we found your horse, but soon after that, the fog cleared enough, then we were able find your trail," Jane said, dismounting. "What is he grinning about?" She pointed at Kahn, whom Cosmos did not even bother closing the eyes of.

"I never asked," Cosmos replied. "His greatest concern seemed to be that the Salaamed sailors would learn their comrades have been taken from their ship and would not sit idle."

"Hmmm…" Jane was thoughtful for a bit. "I wonder if they have had previous encounters or if he feared that just because it was the obvious reaction to them escaping by river. No matter, I will implore them to pursue the captives. After all, some of their own men were taken, it is unlikely they will refuse."

"Where has Moyra disappeared to?" he asked, changing the subject, knowing Jane would not leave her in a situation she deemed unsafe but worried nonetheless.

"She did that sharing-pain trick we have only read about then returned to the inn for some much needed rest. It was amazing. When he started going into convulsions, I thought he would die for sure! I could not shake images of Terry in the worst or the tremors, but then Moyra was there, and he got better," Jane said.

Cosmos knew Jane had recently lost Terry to poison in an abductor attack. Terry was a clever and sophisticated man who was smitten with her. Jane was still emotionally raw and sensitive especially to those inflicted by poison.

Cosmos was surprised to see Echo nodding animatedly in agreement. "Her flesh got goose pimples. She was sweating from concentration, and ripples ran up her back and down her arms, like Moyra's muscles were threatening to go into convulsions," Echo said energetically; he had previously been about to fall asleep and off his horse. "I think she was in worse shape than the poisoned man when she climbed onto Jane's horse and left without a word," Echo concluded.

It sounds like Moyra was in a trance. What if she does not make it back to the Dueling Bard Inn? Cosmos thought franticly.

Cosmos had expected reassurances from them that Moyra was secure and safe or that she would join them momentarily. But Echo's reply in particular only served to make Cosmos more anxious concerning Moyra's well-being. He was more sympathetic to Jane's distress than he had been since their mother died. Not until Moyra did he have anyone to actively care and worry for, thus achieving a level of empathy to understand Jane's feelings.

Their mother's death was especially painful, six years of coughing sickness more of it in bed than out. It seemed like Jane spent more time at her side at that time than Cosmos had the rest of his life combined. Mother would tell Jane of better times before her husband and several of her children had died, and Jane would recount in turn stories of the pond swimming or ice-skating with her many siblings and cousins. Mother's sickness worsened until she was coughing up little pink bits of lung; she died soon after.

Jane had seemed perpetually sad ever since their mother passed away—the everlasting sorrow. Many tried to bring cheer to Jane, but most died dramatically. only adding to her sorrows. Jane immersed herself in swordplay as Cosmos had when their mother first became bedridden. She soon surpassed him at least in single combat for she would get tunnel vision and could not take on multiple opponents as well as he could.

Avigdor turned out to be the one with the antidote to Jane's sorrow—his daughter Moyra, with her infectious smiles and unrelenting charm. He came to the mercenaries guild just after their champion and a group of the guild's best fighters died fighting in King Sebastian Otyugh's vanguard protecting the realm. But it had been a secret conflict, and Derek, as acting guild master, named Jane as champion, upon Avigdor's suggestion, so nobody would know of the nature of the champion's disappearance. The feint worked; anytime someone would ask for the champion's service or when rumors of his demise spread, it was put to them simply that "the champion was currently in the service of Avigdor, the feudal lord to the south." Being Moyra's bodyguard was the best thing for Jane. Cosmos remembered seeing her upon her return and thinking that the two of them looked deliriously happy.

Eclipse his horse whinnied loudly, bringing Cosmos back to the present. He stepped up onto the chariot ready to move on.

"I was going to go back to the inn and make sure Moyra made it to the room safely," Jane started to explain, seeing the worry on Cosmos's face. "But Captain Sanders was taking our sleeping prisoners to the guard tower. Two other guards were going back to join the guards at the city gate, so I asked them to find her instead and make sure Moyra arrived at the inn safely. You were by far in greater danger, so Echo and I moved out after you instead of following Moyra."

CAPTURED

Moyra was used to having many people about her rooms in the mornings—servants starting a fire, setting out attire for her to wear, cleaning up whatever mess was left from the previous day. *Jane*, she thought. Yes, Jane, Moyra's minder, would be about with all these and others, making sure nobody tried to gain entrance into her rooms over the night, making sure that there wasn't anyone suspicious hanging about the alleyways with vantage points to her balcony. Jane, ever diligent, had once jumped from her balcony and chased a man halfway across the city for looking up at her balcony suspiciously. It turned out he was courting her maid and trying to get her attention; they were sweethearts and ended up getting married.

Jane! she tried to say. Panicked but not sure why, Moyra was aware of people about her, but she didn't believe this was her room. She could feel their eyes on her, and they weren't the unobtrusive eyes of servants! *Wake up! Get up!* she thought frantically.

When her body didn't immediately respond, she tried to gather details about where she was and what had happened. *I must be suffering the effects of a trance, but why would I be in a trance? I don't use my wraith in combat. Fighting! There must have been fighting. If I lost someone important to me, the trauma could explain this fugue state,* Moyra thought. Disoriented as she was, Moyra tried to remember if anything bad had happened to her father, fighting at the salt mines with Jane beside Husain, Moyra's father's captain of the guard and unofficial minder.

⌒⌒

Moyra's father knew that Samantha had designs of her own for the salt mines. When he turned down all her advances, Samantha married the leader of a band of sellswords. The sellsword's mob grew, taking in outlaws when they tried to acquire help from the guild of mercenaries. The guild refused and informed Avigdor of the offer. Moyra then begged earnestly of her father to purchase their services instead, but he refused to deal with mercenaries from a position of weakness. He was grateful of the information though and went to their guild personally and attained the services of Jane as Moyra's minder.

Jane refused the title of *minder*, arguing that she wasn't an attendant but a protector, a "bodyguard" and that she would protect Moyra as best she could, regardless of anyone's orders. Moyra was shocked that Jane had proclaimed she wouldn't take orders, but everyone else seemed to think minder and bodyguard were synonyms. Even Moyra's father disagreed with her, claiming she was arguing semantics.

Moyra often tried to make Jane follow Husain's example, but Jane would just laugh at her. Worst, when Jane learned that the only combat training Moyra had was archery, Jane insisted upon beating her into submission for hours every day, calling it sparring. When Moyra went to her father crying about Jane's barbaric rough-and-tumble, he laughed good-naturedly and called it horseplay. Moyra learned there was neither help nor sympathy to be found, so she went into each match, determined to learn all she could. After a few weeks, she could win one in ten rounds of rough-and-tumble or hurly-burly sparring, then Jane switched to cut-and-thrust sparring.

Husain was especially impressed with Jane's blade work; he would talk to her for hours about her techniques. Despite being impressed with Jane's skill, Husain was indisputably better; he won four out of five duels against her. It was hard for Moyra to find amusement there though because Husain said it was just the difference in experience, that Jane was a phenomenal fighter and would soon outshine him. "Whether its speed or power, she's got me beat, but I have a better sense for battle than she does. Her pace gets pulled into my rhythm."

For Moyra, it was like listening to musicians talk about their favorite songs and how to get the strings to play a note just right. Even though they usually spoke of basic moves, she had learned right away; their perfection was many levels too high for her to comprehend they made the ordinary extraordinary. It would also be like artists arguing over how best to use the lighting of a landscape depicted on a great tapestry they intended to make. Moyra felt that if she were an artist, she was surely painting with her fingers, where they each had a hidden accumulation of every size and craft of paintbrush at their disposal.

It was discouraging that after three months of training, Moyra was sure she had improved exponentially but had yet to so much as touch Jane with her blades. Sometimes, her father would give her tips, and Jane would assure her she was improving in leaps and bounds. Whether that was true or not, it was still daunting.

Just about Moyra's only reprieve was laughing at Jane's expense. The servants often teased Jane, calling her a wanton tigress trying to restrain a mate, for chasing Molly's man halfway across the city and bringing him back in ropes. This always made Jane blush scarlet, which only made it all the more enjoyable to tease her. Even the general public throughout the city knew the story; some would tell it that the reason for the haste of the wedding was that the man saw Jane as the alternative to Molly.

Moyra was ashamed of her surly behavior toward Jane and of her intimidation of Jane's overwhelming fighting prowess. She wanted to be encouraged by greatness. Moyra remembered one occasion as a young child when she thanked her father for punishing her for her carelessness. He had been moved to tears and thanked her in turn for understanding that he corrected her in love and not in anger. She didn't believe Jane was a bad person. Moyra found herself wanting to be friends with Jane but didn't think they could grow any closer through their imitation fights.

The next time Jane came to her with bundled-reed practice swords, Moyra refused her cut-and-thrust training but took Jane out to meet some friends instead. They went ridding and hawking, and on their return, they stopped at a sweets shop selling colorful hard candy. That was when Jane opened up to Moyra for the first time telling how she used to dream of getting married, of having a toddler stumbling around the backyard with ducklings following her in close pursuit.

Moyra laughed at the visualization and tried to imagine how Jane would fit into the mental picture. Certainly there was no place for the woman before her dressed in studded leather with a blade on ether hip. Moyra imagined Jane older in one of her mother's long dresses, with her black hair done up in elaborate braids that circled around her head, a sad smile on her face, standing under a cherry tree in full bloom and watching a little girl carrying a duckling in her arms and running from the mother duck chasing her in remonstration, her other babies covered only in down feathers followed in a line.

⌒

Moyra turned her head to the side and opened her eyes, but her vision was blurry and her eyelids heavy, so she let them close. She was still worried about where she was and what was going on, but she was in no condition to do anything about it, even if she could manage to keep her eyes open. So she let oblivion take her thoughts back into dreams of recollection that those answers may come to her.

〜

By this time, the trouble with Samantha and the sellswords was escalating. They had captured a ship and its shipment of salt. They even captured the salt mines for twelve days before Avigdor, Moyra's father, could safely recapture them without endangering the lives of the workers. Once he spread his guards out protecting merchant caravans, ships, mines and mineworkers, Samantha must have deemed Avigdor sufficiently unprotected because she tried to have him assassinated twice.

The first attempt was from six men against Husain and Avigdor on the cobblestone streets not far from home. The commotion alerted Jane and Moyra. By the time they got there, Husain had dispatched two of them. Moyra's father and his minder were holding off the other four but being pushed back wounded. More than a few city dwellers were injured in the initial attack but not badly. Moyra's father limped and held his left hand against his chest staunching the blood flow of a gash.

Avigdor fought with a dagger. Wire handled, it had a wide guard; the *main-gauche* was a good defense against a sword, compared to most daggers. Husain wielded two oversized kukri knives with curved blades that were broader toward the point, not unlike boomerangs in appearance. Moyra grabbed a bow on her way to aid her father but, in her haste, forgot to get a quiver of arrows. Luckily, her father's attackers only seemed to notice the two reinforcements and not the fact that one of them was unprepared; they fled before Jane's deadly blades could reach them.

⌒

Moyra's memories were coming back to her in a flash, but they felt distant, like these weren't the most current events to ensue. Amnesia was very uncommon, but even a temporary fugue could be dangerous. Only about one in two hundred suffered considerable memory loss. But the people around her, the place itself, and even the time of year didn't feel like they match her memory. It was to cool; for one thing, this felt like winter or at least late fall. Moyra wondered how many seasons had passed, thinking about the distant feel of the proceedings. *Could it have been years since these things happened?*

⌒

The second attempt on Moyra's father's life was only by four men, probably from the survivors of the first attempt. Moyra kept a quiver of arrows hanging on her hip most all the time now just because Jane liked teasing her about forgetting them the first time.

The assassins attacked under the cover of darkness. Moyra's father was making plans to inspect the defenses of the salt mine; information gathered suggested the sellswords would try to gain control of them again. Two kicked in the doors of his office, and the other two gained entry from the balcony. Husain was on the balcony. Those two managed to send him over the rail, but he pulled one with him and used his assailant to break his fall.

When Jane and Moyra entered, her father was fighting one man on the balcony; the other two were rushing to join the fight. Moyra's heart dropped—her father didn't have a weapon. He was fending off a sword with his left hand wrapped in a curtain he had pulled from a glass door to the balcony. Suddenly she was losing an arrow she didn't even realize she had pulled from her quiver at her father's attacker. The arrow struck his side; her father hit him in the face with a right hook, sending him over the rail. Jane told the other two confidently that they had failed and that they could live and possibly gain freedom in exchange for information. They dropped their weapons and agreed to be most helpful. Husain soon returned. Avigdor expelled Jane and Moyra from his office.

Moyra was distressed about having killed someone for the first time. The next four or five days were the longest of her life; she didn't sleep much, and when she did, it seemed a turmoil of unrest. Jane spent most of that time with Husain. She would roll her eyes and shake her head at Moyra whenever their eyes met. Her father said he wished she could have lived a long full life without ever having to kill anyone. When she said she wished it was easier, he adamantly said, "No, never that," and that it was a truly unfortunate thing that it became easier each time.

When Moyra's father went to inspect the salt mines, he took Moyra with him, not trusting Samantha to leave her out of their conflict. Just being there raised Moyra's spirits considerably, and Jane seemed happy to spend time in her presence now that she was cheerful.

Curtis L. Gray

Moyra took cover behind a sculpture of a group of belly dancers performing before a fat sultan. The sellswords released crossbow bolts at her and taunted her, saying she joined a harem. It aggravated her to be considered a part of the ugly fat man's group of wives! But they kept firing too much for her to find other shelter regardless of how much it grated her to be there. She was able to fire some arrows of her own and was pleased to see Jane and Husain attack the sellswords. That was when she made the mistake of taking shelter behind a pillar of salt. Two sellswords hid there, obviously trying to move into position to attack her, and Moyra had moved to them! Husain saved her, throwing his weapons at them; each was expertly thrown, and both sellswords died. She looked to him gratefully just in time to see him impaled on the blades of two sellswords while protecting Jane. He also grabbed a large two-handed scimitar by the blade, their leader's weapon, allowing Jane to quickly dispatch all three.

Jane cried over Husain, telling him he couldn't die, asking him how he could be so brainless. He laughed at Jane, touched her cheek, coughed up blood, and told her with a playful grin that she looked stupid. Jane was pale faced and haggard with tears freely flowing. Moyra would never have imagined Jane could look so wretched. Jane told him it was no time to be joking around, and he asked if she was crying because of him. Coughing more, Husain's eyes started to lose their light. He said having both of them depend on him felt pretty nice. Jane said he absolutely could not die and kissed his forehead. He asked if he had ever not done what she told him to even now. Husain said he only did what she told him to do—protecting her with his body. She cried all the more, saying she only told him that greedily so he would stay by her side.

As Jane said that it was all her fault, Moyra knew that wasn't true, knowing that it was actually her fault for moving to the salt pillar. *If I had only continued to give them cover fire from the back of the harem, but no, being the last wife of a kindly old sultan was too good for me, and I'm the reason Husain is dying!* Moyra thought sadly. He died shortly before word of victory came to them.

Moyra's teary eyes opened, revealing to her an unknown room with strange people all around her. "Where am I… what is this place?" she tried to ask, but it came out as a mumble. To her surprise, the room was sandstone, a large obviously man-made cave. Husain's death was sad, but Moyra didn't think it was the cause of her memory loss.

"She is coming to. I thought you said you got her with a sleeping dart? She must have just been knocked unconscious. Otherwise, she couldn't come around this soon." said a youthful man near the cave opening, shaking his head upset. He moved in closer to get a better look at Moyra. Moyra allowed her eyes to close and scrunched up protectively.

"No, she is just having restless sleep. Look here. It was a clean shot. Some people walk in their sleep. Open eyes due to fitful dreams is no big deal," said someone else, lifting her chin and touching a sore spot on Moyra's neck.

Sleeping dart? I have never encountered one of them before, but I don't think that they cause memory loss. Just what have I gotten myself into? Moyra thought sourly.

⌒

Samantha was captured and sentenced to twelve years indenture to the priests of Sands Monastery. Years passed with no more conflicts with the sellswords. Jane and Moyra's friendship grew until they each considered the other their very best and truest friend. Moyra's father was summoned to court at the obsidian throne by King Sebastian Otyugh. Jane was called to another job by the mercenaries guild to deal with the Waif of Chance Harbor. Moyra took the opportunity to go north and see some of the wider world.

That was when the rest of her memories fell into place—of entering the city Brunswick with her new friends, a city plagued by a long line of insidious abductions and murders, a city celebrating in blissful ignorance. Moyra remembered a short embrace with Cosmos ending badly and a restless sleep rudely awakened. She remembered being awakened and led by Jane to join up with Cosmos and Echo. Forming a group, they fought and won against the abductors. Her short-term memory loss was a side effect of being in a trance, like she had first thought. But she hadn't used her wraith in combat; Moyra's empathy for others inhibited that action. No, she used it for healing miraculously; her wraith allowed her to share pain and speed up healing, but the long and strenuous use, combined with the fact that she was already exhausted, caused her to go into a trance.

Of all Moyra's memories the last to return were those of the early morning just after separating with Jane preceding her capture.

On her way back to the inn, half-sleeping, half-awakening, her thoughts and memories blurred and drifted away until Moyra found herself sitting astride an unfamiliar horse in a field with few clumps of grass and red dust of a land farther north than any place she was familiar with. She heard two riders coming up behind her. They spoke to Moyra as they came to a stop on either side of her. But her weariness was such that she didn't make out the words either of them was saying. One of them roughly grabbed the reins from under her horse's neck, pulling them from her hands; she snapped her head up in surprise, eyes popping wide. Moyra instinctively grabbed for her dagger and was surprised to find a small scroll in its sheath instead. They both laughed at her; one even begged her to be reasonable and said that he hated paper cuts the worst. Identifying the emblem on their uniforms, she relaxed and allowed herself to smile before closing her eyes once again.

They escorted her away. Moyra only opened her eyes occasionally each time more befuddled than the last. When they came to a stop, Moyra established the presence of mind to get down from her horse by herself, which seemed to surprise them.

They were at the lowest part of a sandstone cliff. Moyra looked up in wonder as the morning sunlight lighted the cliff face. Few consistent square openings appeared as black holes where the light could not reach.

The sandstone had obviously been labored on for many decades; it looked more like a giant wall or building than any natural occurrence. It was a smooth vertical rise nearly three times the height of the man-made wall surrounding the other sides of the city. Above that, she could see the windswept ledges stuck much farther out, along with jagged crevices with a few weeds and stubborn shrubbery that grow anyplace it could.

That was when she got shot with a sleeping dart. She felt pain in her neck and pulled the dart away, expecting to see a hornet. Moyra didn't see the shooter, but in retaliation of the treachery, she head-butted one man in the nose and stabbed the other with her scroll. *Pity it wasn't a dagger*, she remembered thinking. Moyra turned slapped the horse behind the saddle, sending it running. As she collapsed, she threw the small scroll out after the horse.

Moyra rolled from her back to her side and didn't feel the least bit drowsy but resisted the urge to get up. She had to come up with a plan first and knew that their surprise of the poison wearing off so soon would help her.

"Are you sure she was one of those that took out Rajiv's group? Eight men against four, and two of theirs were women, I just can't believe it. Rajiv alone, discounting his brother, was a better fighter than any four men I have ever known," said a gruff voice.

"Well, I wasn't there anymore than you were, but it sounds like a tall tale a'right. To hear them tell it, we should count ourselves lucky the ship got away," replied the younger man. It sounded to Moyra that he returned to his watch point near the door.

"I have never run into anyone from the mercenaries guild. They're no joke, though, even King Sebastian Otyugh has had occasion to use their services. Three years ago, there was a tale that their champion died saving the king's vanguard," said the gruff speaker ominously.

"That's got to be exaggerated gossip! Their entire guild of mercenaries lead by their champion wouldn't be a match for the vanguard," said the youth. Moyra imagined him waving his arms about animatedly.

"So you would think, but I have an informant who reported vanguard and mercenaries working together to cover up evidence of a conflict with another realm. It seems that the only exaggeration was that of the champion's death. By all accounts, he went south and ended a civil war before it could get blown out across the rest of the realm."

"It's all unconfirmed traveling-merchants boasting, I tell you. Or would you have me believe the latest peddler tale that the champion is actually a woman and that on her return, she stopped to deal with the Waif of Chance Harbor, the suspected werewolf, saving the entire village from infection of that vile curse that's unlikely to be real in the first place," the youth replied sarcastically.

Moyra chose that moment to stand up. She stretched her arms out high and wide, yawning exaggeratedly. The effort of standing revealed that not all the effects of the sleep poison had worn off. "Ah…oh my, Jane really is quite impressive, isn't she?" Moyra asked sardonically as she casually took a book from a wax-covered desk near her. Many candles had burned out on it, leaving the desk looking like something that belonged deep in a limestone cave, wax stalactites nearly reaching the floor where wax stalagmites reached up in conical pillars to meet them at a point.

Smiling, she could almost feel their stunned apprehension at her sudden revival. "I could tell you stories about the champion, though they would mostly just give detail of what you have already heard about her," Moyra said. Turning around, she was glad to see only two people; one was standing in front of a wide opening, which let her discern where they were. They were at the top of one of the granaries built into the wall of the sandstone cliff overlooking Brunswick City. The younger of the two was wearing a gliding suit but without the helmet, so she didn't fear him shooting another dart at her. The other man was standing on top of a trapdoor in the center of the room meant for filling the granaries beneath them. He wore town cloths and would easily blend into a group of people without standing out in any particular way.

"I don't believe it. She must have had some sort of antidote for the sleeping poison and had taken it before I got her with the dart."

The man in the center of the room was already shaking his head. "No. Remember what the guards told you that she healed a poisoned man by using astral projection? Just imagine how much stronger that ability is when used on herself."

Moyra tried her best to give the impression she was relaxed and unperturbed, even allowing the book to fall open in her hands and appearing to have an interest in its contents. Truthfully, she was apprehensive, fearful that she may never escape and see her friends again. She cared not at all for the book's contents nor her captors' argument. When the younger man turned his full attention to the other, Moyra decided that was almost certainly as good a chance as she was going to get.

Closing the book, holding the spine together in both hands, she raised it above her head and threw it with all her might in her arms, back, hips, and legs. Strangely, the weird motion felt completely innate, not unnatural, like her girly throws usually did. The book stayed close, going across the room; the young man ducked at the last instance. Luck was with her; the book opened, causing it to redirect into his face rather than fly harmlessly past. It hit him with a deceptively loud *thud*, betraying the book's light weight. He didn't cry out but exhaled a mist of blood that jetted from his nose and gave the impression that it helped the book propel him from the elevated opening.

The other man turned from her with a stunned expression, only to see a blood mist where his companion had just been. Moyra closed the distance between them, high kicking at his face. He intuitively raised a hand to block but didn't absorb enough momentum to keep it from connecting with her target. The damage was light, but he stumbled several feet away then tripped over his ally's discarded fox-head helmet. She heard a belated cry from the man she knocked from the granary entrance then a loud flapping noise that faded into fluttering and silence, which may have indicated he righted himself and glided to safety. Moyra was surprised to find out that she felt glad it was unlikely she killed the young man. She thought she was becoming more callused to killing, but her relief suggested otherwise or at least that it was a slower progression than she first thought it would be.

"The element of surprise worked well for you, and sure, luck favors the bold," the abductor said in congratulatory tones, and then he took a fighting pose. "But you're sorely mistaken if you think things will keep going your way. I'm sure you're still groggy from the sleep poison. You're not my equal as you are right now. And James didn't die from that fall. He'll glide to the ship and warn them of the Salaamed sailors' pursuit."

Moyra feared he was correct on all counts, but she wasn't about to give up. As her father said, "Just because you will surely lose doesn't mean you shouldn't fight for a just cause." She had no doubt that getting the abductees safely back to their families was a task worth dying in trying to accomplish. "He fell too far to make it to the ship. He'll be lucky to get over the wall. For all we know, he may already be impaled on a spear," Moyra retorted.

"Humph, you know nothing. James will use the great descent to gain far greater speed and new height that would have otherwise been impossible."

Moyra knew he wasn't bluffing. She remembered hawks; oftentimes, the birds would dive low then spread their wings and swoop up and away far faster than they could otherwise fly.

Just then, the cogs and pulleys for the lift outside the opening started turning and squeaking loudly. Moyra used the distraction to gain initiative and attack her opponent, hitting him with a flurry of blows. She feared that those raising the elevator were surely the guards who turned her over to the abductors, returning after seeing an ally depart in daylight, risking their group's exposure. Moyra dodged his attacks and hit him three times every time he tried to hit her. She was under no delusion she would win because he was taking her hits like they were nothing and one of his attacks might well knock her down or out. It happened just like she feared—he hit her with a grazing punch as he came forward. He followed through with his elbow, knocking her to the floor.

Moyra kicked at his knee; he jumped back She grabbed the fox-head helmet he had earlier stumbled over and pulled it over her head. She fired two darts at his face. They hit the beam behind him on either side of his neck. He froze! His fear was a tangible thing. She had to hurry; it would not take long for the elevator to get up to them even as high up as they were. Moyra pointed to the trapdoor in the middle of the room without moving her gaze from him. He took her meaning without a word of protest, moved to the center, opened the granaries deposit door, and jumped in. It was a fifteen-foot drop down to the grain. She slammed the door and tipped the wax cover desk over on top of it.

"Ah, now to get out of here before they return," Moyra said, removing the helmet. She looked around. There was no exit except the opening to the elevator. She thought about cutting the lift ropes but had no tool proficient for the task. Moyra had decided to push the desk out the opening planning to collapse the elevator when she saw another glider suit in the corner. *With that, I may be able to escape. It'll be dangerous and the thrill of a lifetime, plus I don't want to kill anymore than I have to*, thought Moyra. She ran to it. The suit was too big for her, but she didn't mind though; that just made it so that she could put it on more quickly over her armor. After putting on the fox/bat-glider disguise, she scrambled back to the opening, fumbling with the new helmet with her ungainly claws.

Moyra leaped from the opening just in time, barely clearing the heads of those on the lift. She couldn't find her breath for several moments; that time seemed to stop in. Moyra was brought out of her wonderment by a scream that she was surprised to find out was her own. Her scream turned into laughter over her short time in captivity. Laughing in jubilation over her victory against the two and combined with the thrill of being suspended over the city not falling, Moyra considered this a small success but one she had earned all on her own.

She took long steady breaths and searched the horizon for the other glider called James. Not seeing him, she thought that maybe he crashed after all but decided to go on to the abductors ship. If she could manage it, the other ship would need all the help they could get; theirs was much smaller than the abductors' ship and, therefore, would be undermanned come time for the battle.

SAILING AND
SOARING

After reentering the city, Echo begged off to go share the night's events with his friends and family. Some nearby solders were surprised Jane allowed Echo to run off and share information with civilians. Jane just shook her head in annoyance and told them containing the situation was the biggest help they could have given the abductors without actually siding with them. Besides, they had already spread news across half the kingdom that people were being eaten and or cursed to a short life of madness by nightmare monsters that attacked you in the safety of your homes whether you lived alone in the wilderness or in a heavily populated and fortified city. Echo's sharing of the truth about what happened could only bring about favorable events.

The barracks that the sailors were staying in were near the gate. Entertainers from the festival could be found even there vying for coins from travelers. One couple was juggling a half dozen clubs in between each other. Another man was blowing a long length of flame by spewing what must have been the worst-smelling alcohol Cosmos could imagine. Closer to the barracks, a large crowd of people had gathered and were making a lot of commotion. A scantily clad woman was thrown far into the air; she came down kicking and screaming, only to go back up again without a moment's delay.

Jane started running. Cosmos followed, unconcerned. It seemed to be all in good sport, at least from the crowd's reactions. She ran up some steps in front of the barracks, a white stone building, and glared down at them. There were eight big men in the center of the crowd pulling a canvas taut between them. The poor distressed woman was no longer fighting it; she had learned to land on her back, but she was grimacing in pain and holding her wrist protectively.

When Cosmos stopped beside her, Jane pulled one of his daggers and threw it without a moment's hesitation. Just as the woman came to a stop on the canvas, before they could sling her into the air again, the dagger pierced the heavy fabric between her legs. They pulled mightily, rending the canvas in two. The men rolled away from each other, some on to and others under the onlooking crowd. The young woman looked most surprised of all. Because the canvas held her just long enough to set her upright then drop her on her feet.

"Leann!" another woman in tatters yelled, running to the former's side. "Leann, I tried to get them to stop. I'm so sorry I brought you here. Now let's go before they get up!"

Both of the woman's clothes were ripped away to the point of indecency. Her friend grabbed Leann's hand and tried to lead her through the crowd. But too late, one of the men (a sailor) who had been throwing her grabbed Leann's other arm.

"Ouch! Let go, Rachel. It hurts!" In her pain, Leann yelled at Rachel, who held the injured hand, to let go rather than the sailor keeping her from escaping.

"Hey, ham hands, let her go!" Jane yelled at the sailor. Some of the crowd who had already been laughing at the events as they unfolded laughed all the more at Jane's clumsy obscenity. "That sounded better in my head," Jane whispered in irritation so that only Cosmos could hear.

"No kidding?" Cosmos asked sarcastically and couldn't help smirking.

"You should know better than to meddle in the affairs of others," one sailor said, directing his words at Cosmos threateningly. He was holding the dagger that Jane threw, apparently connecting it to Cosmos as the architect of their humiliation.

"He does know better. Now leave the girls and come inside before I'm inclined to embarrass you further in front of all these people," Jane promptly replied before opening the door to the barracks and entering without hesitation. Cosmos waited a moment to see how they would react.

"As if she would be enough to entertain us? Bring them," said the one holding Cosmos's knife. One man with scratches on his face, which Cosmos imagined got them from the women previously trying to escape, rushed to help restrain them and bring them in the barracks. "I've got something that belongs to you," the man holding Cosmos's dagger said, waving it when his attention caught on him silently watching them.

"Then by all means, return it," Cosmos said, turning to follow after Jane. As he entered the barracks Cosmos heard him curse and promise to teach him not to turn his back on him again.

"Well, the men weren't happy with the cold reception we received arriving here. The alcohol is watered down and expensive, not to mention these sleeping arrangements aren't much better than those we endured on the boat," said a tall bare-chested man to Jane. He had the most scars Cosmos had ever seen, but it was unlikely they came from battle or torture as the scars were too neat and evenly spaced.

"Whatever you're here to complain about, you should have come bearing gifts. Your words are unlikely to reach them," Jane replied.

Their conversation ended as the other sailors started noisily coming in behind Cosmos. He kept his back turned to them but didn't miss one of them suddenly going silent and gently walking too close to him. Cosmos quickly turned on one foot, unsheathing a dagger with his right hand; he grabbed a thrusting wrist that had a blade in its hand with his left hand and braced both their weight with his other leg. He slammed the handle of his dagger into the man's elbow hitting the funny bone and nerves that control grip then easily pulled his dagger from the sailor's hand.

Curtis L. Gray

"Pete, you would stab a man in the back?" asked the man next to Jane in an accusatory voice. Cosmos stepped back then sheathed his daggers, walking toward Jane.

"I wasn't going to hit his vitals. Just returning his dagger, I was," replied his would-be attacker stupidly, rubbing his elbow and funny bone with a pained grin on his face.

"Why are you two here?" Jane asked the two women as though it was their choice to be dragged into the barracks.

"My husband was taken by the monsters," said the one Cosmos identified as Rachel. "The guards just said, 'Everything that could be done was being done.' So we came down here trying to enlist the help of more sympathetic people. I never imagined we would find such callused and uncaring attitudes toward our plight."

"This trouble of monster attacks is your affair and none of ours. Why should we help your city when we are not even welcome here?" Pete asked distastefully.

"The abductors have been taking their captives to the big ship that was at the docks when you arrived. It left last night. Do you think you can catch it?" Jane asked the disfigured man next to her.

"Why don't you try making us? I'll die before helping this ungracious city," Pete said, coming up to Jane threateningly.

Before he could react, Jane slapped the flat of her sword against his face, resting the point just beneath his eye. The swift action surprised everyone, and her blade drew blood in his skin along both edges up to the point. "I'm not against drawing blood, but getting someone

I've killed to do what I want them to seldom works as well as I'd like," Jane replied coldly.

"Pete, you moron! They are assassins, and you're practically begging them to kill you! I'm surprised your guts aren't decorating the floor after attempting to put a blade in his back," the man disfigured by decretive scars upbraided his fellow sailor.

"That's okay. I wanted my dagger back, and what better place to give a dagger back than in the back?" Cosmos asked playfully. They both look at him like he was crazy, and Jane shook her head in annoyance of the bad joke.

"We are not here asking for your help—" Jane said trying to explain the situation but was interrupted.

"Is that so? Then you must be going to say you're here to demand it. Am I right?" Pete said hostilely, but now he stepped away from Jane, not about to endanger himself without the support of his allies. Retreating didn't lower his hostility; if anything, a menacing atmosphere seemed to rise. It was surprisingly subtle and fast; the change came before Cosmos knew it. Looking around, he saw many of the sailors had found knives, clubs, or makeshift weapons from whatever was around them. One man simply wrapped a thick rope around his arm many times from fist to armpit. They did not seem the type to lose a barroom brawl no matter how dirty they had to play.

"Not at all, I just thought you would want your friends back that they captured," Jane said, unconcerned by their change to hostility.

"You're not fooling anyone. We are all here.

They haven't taken any of us," Pete said with an air of superiority.

"You are making fools of your selves. She is obviously talking about the men on our ship," the scar-covered man said, pulling a club from one man's hand and knives from two others. "Of course, we will go after them. Not even this scruffy lot of misfits would leave their comrades in our enemy's hands."

Everyone seemed to agree with him. They started gathering their things. One pair was already out the door running toward the city gates and presumably their ship.

"At least one of you should come with us. We will need all the information we can get about these monsters," the scar-covered man said.

"Now hold on just a minute. There has to be another option other than these two!" Pete started to complain, wiping the last of the blood from his face. New blood surfaced, but it congealed and didn't run down his face.

"Take me and five of my men to replace those that were taken!" Captain Sanders said from the doorway. "I have been interrogating prisoners all night. They talked soon enough after the threat of using their own poison on them. So I know better where they are going than these two do anyway."

Many people voiced their agreement of taking the city guards with them, as they made ready to abscond.

"He is correct. I don't know where they are going, and I already shared with him what I know of the abductors," said Jane.

Cosmos and Jane left the barracks escorting Leann and Rachel back to the residential area of Brunswick. Rachel helped him get the injured Leann onto the back of his horse then rushed to climb up behind Jane. Leann held her injured hand protectively against her stomach and clutched tightly to him with her other arm. He followed Jane, guided by her passenger, away from the main streets toward the natural wall of the city. Cosmos was surprised of how conscious he was of Leann; he could clearly feel her warm chest pressed against his back even through his armor. A few times during the short ride, his eyes drifted to her exposed legs.

"Why is your heart beating so fast? It's enough to make me anxious," Leann asked, pulling tighter to him with her good hand, which was indeed directly over his heart, and looking over his shoulder into Cosmos's eyes.

"Well…ah…umm," Cosmos tried to reply, but his words abandoned him, looking into her eyes so close to his own. He could feel his cheeks heat up, and her eyes seemed to smile. Though he could not see her mouth pressed against his shoulder, he imagined a big mischievous grin. He turned face front and felt her silent chuckles vibrate through them before she loosened her grip slightly.

He was relieved when Jane pulled to a stop ahead of him and Rachel jumped down. Leann took the hand he offered and slid down with a great big smile that made him blush. Rachel looked from Leann to Cosmos and back again with an unasked question on her face. Jane laughed lightly, and Cosmos kicked his horse into motion; after looking back at Leann, he decided her pale skin and body build was about the same as Moyra's.

"I am glad we did not have to go downriver with the sailors," Cosmos said before Jane could tease him further once he pulled up beside her. He had seen her silently mouth the words "I'm sure you are" before replying sincerely.

"Yes, me as well. Captain Sanders showed up at an opportune time, but I had no intention of following the abductors in that manner." Jane replied and smiled when Cosmos looked at her and turned his head to one side as if to ask in what manner she did intend to follow. "After last night's raid, I am sure they have been attacking from inside the city. Look at the cliff face. Those sandstone walls are the city's storage of supply. I will have the guards check all of them for any sign of the abductors. We will take the gliders I brought with me up there and pursue them from above."

Cosmos and Jane looked up at the unnatural holes in the city's one natural wall just in time to see a headless giant bat fall from one of them. They simultaneously kicked their horses into a run, riding to where it would crash, but before it could crash, it righted itself and started gliding. Cosmos then noticed that it was not headless, just that the abductor simply was not wearing the oversized bat-head helmet. The abductor's downward arc brought him dangerously close to the ground before he started rising at incredible speed. Just before he swooped past Jane and Cosmos, they saw his blood-covered face. As they turned to watch him pass, there was a sickening smack, and they both closed their eyes with pained expressions, not daring to look, realizing he did not gain enough height to clear the building. The abductor smashed into the wall under the balcony of the top floor of the building next to them.

"Eww! I would like to think that was painless," said Jane.

Cosmos was speechless. He felt a cold sweat go over him, thinking that if even an abductor crashed, what chance did they have of successfully using the gliders?

Two city guards came running around the corner but skidded to a stop upon seeing Jane and Cosmos. Jane raised an eyebrow suspiciously then told them in a commanding voice that allowed no compromise, "We are going up to the opening. He came out of show us the way." As usual when Jane took command, people fell into her pace.

The guards lead them briskly to a creaky old elevator directly beneath the opening. At the base of the sand-stone wall was a small enclosure with a cheap straw roof and equally cheap wood slat walls. There was room in the enclosure for a wagon to be backed up against the wall, where there was a floodgate built into the wall, with a sluice-box-like arm, to hold and control the release of the wall's contents. By the looks of the grain-covered floor and sacks in the corner of the room, this particular storage catch was a granary. Jane didn't even have to tell the guards to man the ropes and pulleys; they took their places ready to lift the four of them. As they raised the group, Cosmos tried to help, but Jane held him back saying that there was only room for two to work and urged them faster.

About halfway up, they could hear a struggle going on in the room above the granary. The guards stopped working the elevator. Cosmos urged them to go faster than ever, but they just looked at each other as though each was asking the other what to do. Jane pulled her sword and gave them a level look; whether they took the look as encouragement or a threat, they worked the elevator with renewed vigor. Either the creaky old elevator was now too noisy to hear the conflict above or it was settled because they could no longer hear anything, even though they were much nearer the opening.

"Look there!" Cosmos said to Jane, who was still "encouraging" the guards to go faster. Pointing to the opening where he had seen movement, just as Jane looked up, a giant fox-bat leap from the opening. Cosmos swept his cloak in front of himself and Jane just before it leaped, in case it tried to shoot them with poison darts. There was a scream that shocked him almost as much as the laughter that followed after it ended.

"Moyra!" he yelled automatically, somewhat unconsciously unbelieving. *Moyra,* he thought, mind reeling. *How could she be here now? I can recognize that laugh anywhere no matter what disguise it wears, that has to be her.*

The guards stopped again! Cosmos looked at them, angry for the delay when Moyra was so close but now leaving at incredible speed as she glided far from his side. He was surprised to see one guard had taken up his spear, only to have Jane's blade freeze him in place as it rested on his neck. The other guard stood with his hands held high, trying to assure her he would attempt no such folly.

"I recognize you now! You're the guards I sent to make sure Moyra safely returned to the inn," Jane said accusingly, then drew a line of blood at his neck, and he responded by dropping his spear. "She was in a trance from helping your fellow guard, but you betrayed her by delivering her to your sinister masters instead of helping her."

"How many of your friends are in here?" Cosmos asked, pointing his thumb to the opening Moyra fled from.

"Two," said the guard, holding his hands high, then he looked down toward the building that the abductor crashed into. "Well, one now."

"Shut up!" the other said, but Jane slapped her sword against his jaw, reminding him that she was in charge of the situation. Cosmos didn't hesitate; he took two fast steps toward the wall then jumped and took three more scrambling steps up its sandstone surface and grabbed the bottom of the opening.

"Wait! They always attack in groups of six there could be five more in there!" Jane tried to reason with him urgently.

Whatever the situation turned out to be, Moyra had managed to get a glider disguise on and escape, so he didn't think it likely that he would be attacked going in. As he pulled himself up and into the room, he expected to see at least one person dead or incapacitated. There was a little bit of blood on the floor where he climbed up, just speckles, nothing severe. A book lay open, its pages crumpled, and there was a bed in one corner near an overturned desk, along with excessive amounts of broken wax and an abandoned fox-head helmet from the abductor's giant-bat disguise, but he could not see the other abductor he had expected to find.

As he cautiously moved closer to the overturned desk, he half-expected to find someone hiding behind it, ready to attack him, but there wasn't anyone there or anywhere to be seen. He heard the creaking of ropes and pulleys raising the elevator the last two meters. At the same time, he felt thumping on the trapdoor beneath his feet. Cosmos bent to right the desk; it was heavier than it looked. The desk still had great clumps of wax stubbornly clinging to the top and sides, and just before he finished standing it upright, they fell free. With the heavy mounds of wax no longer attached, he overexerted, noisily throwing the desk on its far side.

"Get her!" he heard a guard yell from outside of the elevator, followed by a ruckus and the clang of steel on stone. Cosmos feared the noise he caused had allowed them to attack Jane in a moment of distraction; he rushed to help her.

"Don't try anything stupid!" Jane yelled as Cosmos came out onto the elevator. "I don't want to have to kill both of you." One man was motionless on the floor; the other was also on the floor but hanging halfway off the elevator, clinging desperately and urgently trying to get back up. "I said don't," she repeated, swinging her sword a good three feet over his head.

"Don't kill me," the guard pleaded.

Jane looked down in surprise as though she didn't see him.

"Jane?" Cosmos asked, concerned.

She turned toward him, her face covered in yellow blinding powder. Soothingly, Cosmos said, "Step back. He's just trying to get back up." Then he rushed to the guard and pulled him up and slammed him facedown. He saw that the dead guard's hand was yellow and easily imagined the conflict that transpired. They heard the trapdoor hinge open. "Put your weight on him. I have to get back in there." She reached her hand out, and he took it, directing it to the guard's head. Jane plopped down on his back and slid her sword under the guard's neck as Cosmos rushed back inside.

The man coming out of the granary was surprised to see Cosmos but reacted fast stretching out toward the abductor helm. Cosmos leapt, closing the distance. He swung his sword; the fox-head helmet went onto his head, pointing at Cosmos's face. His sword touched the nose just in time to redirect the shots. The first shot impacted on his chest; the second went wide. The abductor dropped like a sack of potatoes. Cosmos was so surprised he almost let him fall back down into the grain below. He grabbed an arm and pulled the limp body back up then removed the mask/helm and confirmed that he was unconscious. When Cosmos hit the snout with his sword, he must have forced the abductor's head and neck around too far causing, a knockout.

Cosmos looked around the room, hopeful of finding another glider disguise to pursue Moyra, but with no such luck. So he focused on what he could do. There was a pitcher in a large bowl on a nightstand. He went to it; Jane would need to wash her eyes out soon to avoid long lasting damage to them. The bowl was empty, and the pitcher was only one quarter full. Taking the pitcher and dragging the abductor out onto the elevator by the collar of his shirt, Cosmos said, "I've got some water for your eyes. Look up." After washing her eyes with the little water available, Jane made as though to go in the room. "There is nothing in there, we will have to go and get your gliders if we are going to purse her," Cosmos said urgently.

Jane looked at him in surprise. "You have tunnel vision whenever it comes to Moyra. We are not pursuing her. What we are trying to do is stop these abductions!" Jane said sternly, walking up to him and pulling the dart that shot him from his chest armor. "What if there were five of them?" Jane held the dart up for him to see; he knew she meant abductors and not darts.

"She was escaping from the returning guards not anyone in that room," Cosmos defended.

"Sure, but even if you knew that then, you didn't care at all for your own safety or mine when you went in there!" Jane retorted.

Cosmos felt ashamed looking at her pained red eyes and yellow powder smeared face.

"I'm at fault for allowing myself to be distracted, but you should think of how your actions will affect other people besides simply Moyra. Their taking a ship full of people away, and they had no intention of stopping there. Moyra is new to this, but even she can see the bigger picture. That's why she didn't simply escape but continued along the river after the abductors' ship. I had to draw you into this by using Moyra to lure you. Otherwise, you would have simply went south in pursuit of your own interests. You didn't even come on my last job when I asked you too, and I sorely needed your help."

"Well…I sent Terry…he insisted…besides… Moyra—" explained Cosmos, or he tried to, but Jane threw her hands up exasperated.

"Let's leave the past in the past, but right here and now, I need you—they need your help." Jane waved a hand to indicate the city or maybe she was gesturing toward the river and the people held captive on the abductors' ship. "Don't go being overly careless. Moyra is out of immediate danger, and even if she wasn't—and there are gliders here ready for us to use—we couldn't leave without setting certain things in motion here in the city."

Cosmos was surprised to find how much more selfish he was than Jane. Even now after hearing her lecture, all he could think about was the hole that would be left in his chest if something happened to Moyra, that she would no longer able to occupy that space. That didn't bear thinking about! For Moyra surely inhabited a place within him that was greater than the entirety of his being, and not going to her rescue felt like it would surely cause him to implode. Yet Jane, whose life was a long list of those she had loved and lost, was optimistically thinking of how best to help others who held no emotional attachments to her, unlike her best friend, Moyra, whom she surely loved as much as a sister.

Jane sighed and said, "I'll only be a moment," seeing the worry on his face. She hurried into the room.

Cosmos instructed the captive guard not to move from his facedown position. He then searched the unconscious captive, only finding a lock pick, a fake mustache, and a small coin pouch. When Jane returned, holding a small scroll, she pulled a matching one out of her belt pouch. Cosmos had one prisoner's hands tied behind his back and both hobbled so they couldn't run once they got to the ground. The conscious guard captive waited with his hands untied, ready to help lower the elevator.

"I found this at the base of the wall. I think it's the scroll Moyra picked up in the night," Jane said, indicating the small scroll she pulled out of her belt pouch. "She must have lost it in the struggle trying not to be captured. These are quite common scrolls, so it may have nothing of value or they may each have valuable information that will help us end this."

"It's nothing," the guard said, reaching into his belt pouch. He gave Jane a third scroll to match the first two. "We sometimes get orders from Captain Sanders on just such scrolls."

"I'll decide that for myself," Jane replied, unrolling all three.

Cosmos was interested in what the scrolls held but was more worried about Moyra and the danger she may be getting into and didn't want her to be all alone. He and their captive guard took the elevator down as fast as they could.

"This scroll that Moyra had is golden. I think it was meant for that guy you killed on the bridge!" Jane said excitedly. "What was his name—Kahn?" She seemed to ask to indicate it was for the abductor named Kahn of the two people Cosmos killed on the bridge, not that she had actually forgotten his name because she didn't even look up from the scroll that she considered to be holding golden information. "This has the names of their rats hidden in the city guard's ranks. No way! There is even mention of someone they have among the city councilmen."

"Damn! It's all over if you have that," the bound abductor solemnly said, struggling to sit up. "That was meant to keep us in business even after the game of us pretending to be wild animals was up."

"What does he mean?" Cosmos asked when the abductor fell silent, and Jane simply smirked as though the scroll confirmed what he said.

"Now that it is common knowledge that the abductors are not supernatural demons cursing people to agonizing deaths or animals, winning easy prey, but are men capturing people, it would be obvious they had guards helping them with their human trafficking. This scroll shows that they were going to turn greedy guards who didn't know much about them over to us to take the heat off their other guards and make us complacent. They even had plans to make it look like Captain Sanders was helping them." Jane picked up the other two scrolls in one hand for Cosmos to see. "One of these has the guard captain's forged signature and bogus orders he would never give. They have been playing him for a fool this whole time, with guards like them hindering all his efforts," Jane said in conclusion as she nodded toward the dead guard and pointed the scrolls in her hand at the guard helping lower them.

"Hey, I'm trying to help you. I only sided with them out of fear for my family. I would have been the first one they betrayed, but they would have killed me rather turn me over to you," the guard said, trying to better his standing as their captive, but Jane gave him an icy glare that reminded his that he just turned her best friend over to his detestable masters.

"Once we get down, hurry and get the gliders. I'll wait for you here assigning guards tasks on how I want them to continue without us," Jane instructed to Cosmos.

At the bottom, many guards were waiting for them. Turlock among them; he was surprised to see one guard dead and the other held as a prisoner.

"What is the meaning of this?" Turlock demanded. Cosmos pushed through the gathering without pause or explanation.

"It should be common knowledge by now that some guards have been helping the abductors," Jane replied, handing Turlock two scrolls. "Some by choice and many more in ignorance, just following orders, your captains orders, or so they thought. Which of these was written by Captain Sanders, and which is a forgery made by the abductors? Can you tell?"

"They both have his name on them," Turlock said as though that clearly meant they were from his captain and shouldn't be questioned further.

"Yes, but one has very questionable orders. These are common scrolls used throughout the city, not just by you guards, but that's all the more reason to have suspicion. It isn't like you use special scrolls that not just anyone could get their hands on, not to mention it should be clear they were not written by the same person," Jane explained, her voice fading away as Cosmos rode back toward the Dueling Bard Inn.

Along the way, Cosmos found some people trying to capture Jane's horse, Alabaster, but the ebony
horse refused to let them grab his reins, much less
ride him. He remembered that Moyra was supposed
return to the inn on Jane's black horse. *She must have
sent him running, trying to leave any sign of her capture,*
Cosmos thought.

As he returned to the stable of the inn, Alabaster in
tow, the door banged open, revealing a very distraught
Avilla. Tears streaking down her cheeks she moaned.
"They got Gabriel, along with Caleb and my brother.
We have to do something!"

The raw emotion in her voice brought a lump to his
throat. He could hear a horse coming fast; he turned
away from her before tears could form in his eyes. It
was Echo, who rode in asking questions before he came
to a stop. "Where is Jane? Is Moyra finally here? I rode
down to the barracks looking for you all." He spoke in
a rush and would have kept going if Cosmos didn't say
something to interrupt him.

"They got her," Cosmos said, hardly taking note of
Echo's disbelieving face as he got down from his horse
and started to go into the inn.

"Oh! Poor Moyra, what do we do?" Avilla asked,
throwing her arms around Cosmos's neck and pulling him tight to her chest from her vantage point in
the doorway.

"Moyra? What about Jane?" Echo asked, quickly
getting down and joining them at the door.

By the time, Cosmos got over his surprise of being
embraced and finished untangling himself from Avilla.

"Gliders, Jane wants to follow them with her gliders," Cosmos said quickly, moving across the inn's common room.

"Brilliant!" was Echo's only reply as he sprinted after Cosmos. Avilla took a deep breath then followed them too.

As Cosmos explained to them how Moyra was captured and subsequently freed herself, he had no thoughts of dissuading them from coming along because their friends were captured too. He pitied anyone who would try and stop him from going to Moyra's aid, but he did tell them about the abductor crashing into a building— full disclosure just so they could make up their own minds without feeling like he was encouraging them to take a potentially fatal path.

"I hate that they have guards helping them. It makes joining the Spearwielder Guard seem somehow dirty," Avilla said scornfully, after hearing of the guards who betrayed Moyra.

"That's not on you, Avilla. You haven't accepted bribes. You joined to make a difference, and now you can," her brother said encouragingly.

"I haven't even been offered a bribe. Who knows, they may have been able to compromise me with the right leverage most anyone is susceptible," Avilla reasoned.

"Echo, you carry those three. I'll carry these three, and Avilla will bring the helmets," Cosmos said while separating the gliders into two piles and then giving Avilla a burlap sack full of fox-head helmets. "You're right about anyone being susceptible to bribery."

Cosmos decided to give an example when Echo cast a doubting look. "Most guards almost certainly didn't know the person bribing them was an abductor, and maybe the bribe was disguised as something besides the obvious. Let us say you're a guard on duty at the gate and you're getting hungry, but your shift doesn't end for another hour. Now you know you can't just let anyone take over for you without permission, but another guard a friend says he will watch the gate for you while you run grab a bite to eat. A favor from a friend can hardly be considered a bribe unless during the short time you're away, the abductors take a wagonload of prisoners out of the gate you were supposed to be watching. Even if you couldn't be persuaded by someone offering any amount of gold or threatening your life, the fact you were bribed would remain." Cosmos finished up the tale just as they left the inn. He was pleased to see that it seemed to sober the younger man of some of his naivety.

He soon returned to the elevator with Echo, Avilla, all six glider-bat suits, and their fox-head helmets as well. Jane was reading scrolls, and an old guard was giving his fellows orders with concerned looks to Jane now and then just to make sure she wasn't disgruntled with anything he told them to do. Jane exclaimed at how fast he returned and welcomed Echo and Avilla to come along even before they told her of their friends' capture. She chose two nervous guards to use the other two gliders; they didn't like it, but with an explosive outburst from the older guard, they were suddenly all too happy to oblige. Cosmos liked him immediately and was pleased Jane found someone suitable to leave in charge. Turlock and another big man pulled at random from an onlooking crowd of people to put to work raising the elevator as the six of them put on their glider disguises.

"This is all of our first time. I would like to say 'Follow my lead, but the truth is I want to see each of you go first and I will imitate whoever has the most success," Jane said and was genuinely surprised at their indigent looks and unsatisfied replies.

"Are you saying that it does not matter whatever happens to us as long as you learn from our failures?" asked one guard angrily.

The other agreed, saying, "That was exactly what she meant!"

"No! Not at all, I would much prefer to learn from your success," Jane said reassuringly.

Avilla let out a nervous laugh and looked as though she was about to cry.

"Jane is saying that the abductors are a long ways away, and we should all think for ourselves how best to gain the height, distance, and speed needed to catch up to them, not to simply follow each other misguidedly, as one blind man trying to lead another," Echo said defensively as though in setting right their misunderstanding, he was protecting Jane's honor.

"I'll go first," Cosmos volunteered, which seemed to put the guards at ease. He got the impression that they feared being pushed off the edge only to find they had faulty gliders as punishment for their fellow guards' betrayal.

Calmness came over Cosmos, and by the time the elevator made its record time to the top, he was just putting on his helmet. He was the first to jump from the elevated position. Without any hesitation, he leaped and dived twenty meters before pulling out of the dive. He knew that diving and gaining as much speed as he could would be his only chance to catch up to Moyra before she reached the abductors' ship. It was surprising how wide the hinged wings would open and gave him the feeling of being much larger. Looking over his shoulder, he watched the others follow his lead, though only Jane dared dive; the other four hovered high and slow. Cosmos would have liked to see everyone go first too, but he volunteered because he wasn't about to wait for them to gather the nerve first.

Not being able to flap their wings like real animals, he feared they would all constantly lose height. But warm air came off the city below, gently raising him with it, and by the time he and Jane crossed over the city wall, they had regained their former height. The other four were far higher still, though they seemed to still be where they started other than gaining much more height. Cosmos wondered if they had a better chance of catching up to Moyra with their added height but took some comfort in that Jane followed his method.

A half an hour later, he had yet to catch a glimpse of Moyra's glider, but he could see the white sails of a ship going downriver, probably the ship with Captain Sanders onboard. Later about the same time, he could clearly make out the lower part of the ship. He caught a hint of Moyra's glider, but it was below the horizon and hard to make out among the foliage. Looking over his shoulder, Jane had fallen back quite a ways and was a great deal higher than him. He had to look over his shoulder many more times before he spotted the other four. They were just specks, and he had a hard time trying to convince himself that they weren't actually birds. Cosmos had gained on Moyra quite a bit and could even make out the white sails of a second ship larger than the first.

He estimated that Moyra was somewhere in between the two ships but that she wouldn't catch the abductors' ship before losing too much height and would be forced to land. At that time, a strong tailwind came up, forcing him a little higher but much faster than he had gone so far. Flight became rough with the arrival of stronger winds irregular and unpredictable, very unlike the smooth gliding they had enjoyed that morning. Cosmos had a frightening image of a kite getting away from a child in strong wind; only he pictured himself as the kite soaring out of control.

Much to his surprise, the abductors' ship lowered their sails, slowing so Moyra could catch up. He wasn't surprised that they were allowing Moyra to catch up; obviously, they thought she was one of their own. But in slowing for her, the other ship would surely catch them up as well. Surely they recognized it as the Salaamed sailor's ship from which they killed or captured several men, so as careful as they might have been, they had to be at least considering the possibility of an attack.

Even with the abductor's ship slowing, Moyra was about to touch down in the river, much to Cosmos's distress. He thought that when she hit the river, she would indubitably drown. It was no easy task getting into the giant fox-bat-glider suit on dry land, how much harder it would be to get out of it soaking wet in the surge of the river? If she drowned, his heart would surely sink with her; luckily, it didn't come to that. The same wind he was fighting with finally reached her, and she rose abruptly. Cosmos sighed audibly, and it felt like his heart only just then started beating again after several moments of holding still.

The wind sent the ship carrying Captain Sanders and his city guardsmen swiftly sailing directly at the abductors' ship. That, combined with Moyra soaring over the railing and sending a barrage of poison darts at anything that moved, put everyone onboard in a panic. Three city guards manning a large harpoon gun fired a harpoon into the rudder of the larger ship, which rendered steering impossible.

Cosmos laughed as he came into earshot because he heard Moyra shout, "Here is a taste of your own medicine!" She circled the ship twice, gaining height before she ran out of darts, and they started returning fire with arrows. At which point, Moyra steered off toward land, which wasn't far away, thanks to the malfunctioning rudder. Two arrows hit her left wing, only making small holes, but they soon ripped, making it impossible to glide properly. Cosmos fired darts at the archers as fast as he could from a great distance away; he hit one of the archers a minimum of three times, and three others jumped overboard, but he doubted that he hit any of them. As he turned off to follow Moyra, Jane swooped past him, firing her darts more sparingly.

There was a loud *crash* and *bang*, followed by the splintering of wood, which made him turn back despite his worry for Moyra. *Will the ship sink, drowning all those*

Curtis L. Gray

captives despite our best efforts to rescue them? Cosmos thought, stricken with fear for their well-being.

The ship stopped and gave the illusion of going backward as the river flowed past, then it started moving again, turning sharper inland and riding up on the dirt and gravel bank. The other ship dropped anchor, and men desperately dived over the railing into the river, swimming for what Cosmos didn't know until he saw from his elevated height—people flowing downriver from the far side of the larger ship. At least a dozen people came out of what must be a great big hole in the ship. He hoped that they weren't affected by sleeping poison, incapacitated from the crash, or otherwise unable to swim for safety.

Cosmos saw Moyra near a lone standing rock as he searched for a place to land, but he failed to see three archers abandoning their doomed ship on the hunt for people of whom to exact their vengeance. The first arrow hit his left leg above the knee; the pain was unparalleled he almost blacked out. A few seconds later after the initial shock, the pain was manageable, but it was too late—the next two arrows had already hit his left glider wing. Remembering the abductor who crashed with an arrow in his back and broke his own neck from his helmet hitting the ground wrong, Cosmos shock his helmet loose just before he crashed so that the same thing wouldn't happen to him.

His crash wouldn't have been so bad, sliding across the gravel on his stomach, if not for the arrow stuck in his leg. The arrow broke right away, but it still felt like it must have hit every rock possible as he skidded to a stop. Vision blurry, only scarcely holding on to consciousness, he saw Moyra running toward him. He wanted to warn her away, but he couldn't manage to get the words out. She ran past him and took up his abandoned helmet. Firing darts at the archers, they scattered. She fired rapidly, but apparently she was having trouble aiming because only one archer went down by the time she was out of darts.

The archers came at them, taking their time to get the perfect shot. Moyra abandoned the helmet and meekly walked to Cosmos's side. As they approached, a shadow descended on them, and both archers fell on their faces with a dart in each of the backs of their necks.

"Thanks, Jane," Cosmos and Moyra said together without looking up, too silent for the glider who passed by to hear. She then grabbed the arrow in Cosmos's leg and, with three mighty tugs, jerked it free, freeing him of consciousness at the same time.

<hr>

Gabriel, Gemini, and Caleb had been working with the captive sailors in order to think up a plan on the ship to fight back against the abductors. Their plans hadn't developed much when the ship slowed and then came under attack, but their efforts surely helped keep many captives safe and expedited their escape.

From the wrecked ship, all known captives were freed along with many people whom weren't even suspected of being missing. There were many injuries, and a few people nearly drowned, but thanks to the efforts of Capt. Sanders and the sailors, no captives died. It was discovered that the abductors were from another continent, where they took tourists and all manner of foreigners as slaves; their government was cracking down on them, so they sought new captives from distant inconspicuous lands as they'd done in the distant past.

Back in the City of Brunswick, great efforts were made to bring to justice the abductors and all those who had helped the would-be captors. Among those tried were a handful of guards, two bandit groups, and a city council official.

Two days later, Cosmos Sorrow and Moyra Sublime rode away from the Dueling Bard Inn toward her desert homeland, feeling fulfilled and happy just to be in each others company, they were content.

"What are we going to do next?" Moyra asked. She looked in the opposite direction to which Jane rode with Echo at her side; Echo's hair was growing back white over the scare the boomerang gave him. *Those twins will never be so easily confused for one another again.* She mussed to herself. "Oh I expect we will find excitement aplenty no matter what we do," she said, answering her own question. Out of the four who decided to join The Spearwielder Guard, only Gemini stuck with the decision. Moyra thought that had more to do with the city girl named Leann than a desire to be apart of the army; Leann was stuck to Gemini's arm every time she saw them. Moyra was sure Leann came to the inn looking for Cosmos, but Mephitis easily dissuaded her without Moyra ever saying a word. As for Mephitis's daughters, they returned to the family ranch with Gabriel and Caleb in tow.